DAVE DAWSON
AT
DUNKIRK

by
R. SIDNEY BOWEN

THE WAR ADVENTURE SERIES

THE SAALFIELD PUBLISHING COMPANY
AKRON, OHIO * NEW YORK

Dave Dawson

Republished, and reedited from the public domain.

**ISBN-13:
978-1522891956**

**ISBN-10:
1522891951**

CONTENTS

CHAPTER

I HITLER GIVES THE ORDER!
Page 5

II DIVING DOOM
Page 11

III DAVE MEETS FREDDY FARMER
Page 19

IV PRISONERS OF WAR!
Page 25

V IN THE ENEMY'S CAMP
Page 33

VI THEY'LL NEVER BEAT US
Page 41

VII SHOOT!
Page 49

VIII ESCAPE!
Page 57

IX A DESPERATE MISSION
Page 65

X TRAPPED IN WAR SKIES!
Page 73

XI FIGHTING HEARTS
Page 81

XII IN THE NICK OF TIME
Page 93

XIII BOMBS FOR NAMUR
Page 101

XIV ORDERS FROM HEADQUARTERS
Page 109

XV BELGIUM GIVES UP!
Page 119

XVI FATE LAUGHS AT LAST
Page 127

XVII THUNDER IN THE WEST
      Page 137

XVIII WINGS OF DOOM
      Page 145

XVIII THE WHITE CLIFFS!
      Page 153

CHAPTER ONE

Hitler Gives The Order!

The first thing Dave Dawson saw when he woke up was the combination clock and calendar on the little table beside his bed. He stared at it sleepy eyed and tried to remember why he had put it where he would see it the very first thing when he opened his eyes. He knew there was some reason, an important one, but for the life of him he couldn't remember.

He struggled with the problem for a moment or two and then sat up in bed and glanced about the room. For one brief second the unfamiliar sight startled him. Then he realized where he was and grinned broadly. Sure enough! This was his room in the Hotel de Ney in Paris, France. This was just a little part of the wonderful dream that had really come true!

The "dream" had begun two weeks ago. It had begun with the thundering roar of the *Dixie* Clipper's four engines that had lifted Dave and his father from the waters of Port Washington Bay, Long Island, on the first leg of the flight across the Atlantic to Lisbon, Portugal. His father had been sent to Europe on a government mission, and after much coaxing and pleading had consented to take Dave along. The thrill of a lifetime, and during every minute of these last two weeks Dave Dawson had been living in a very special kind of Seventh Heaven.

To fly to a Europe at peace was something, but to fly to a Europe at war was something extra special. It was a trip a fellow would remember all the days of his life. It was an adventure that he'd tell his grandchildren all about some day. The Clipper roaring to a landing at Bermuda, then on to the Azores, and then farther eastward to Lisbon. The train journey across Portugal to Spain, then up across Spain and over the Pyrenees into France. Finally on to Paris and all the beautiful things that beautiful city had to offer.

Not all of the things, however, had been beautiful. There were lots of things that were grim looking and made a fellow think a lot. The things of war. True, the war was a long, long ways from Paris. It was far eastward between the great Maginot Line of the French and the Siegfried Line of

Adolf Hitler's Nazi legions. There it had remained for eight months, now, and people were saying that there it would remain. Hitler would never dare attack the Maginot Line, and eventually the war would just peter out.

Yes, that was the talk you heard all over Paris, but the grim things were there for you to see with your own eyes just the same. The batteries of anti-aircraft guns strategically placed about the city. The fat sausage balloons that could be sent up to great heights as a barricade against raiding German bombers, should Hitler ever decide to send them over. Then too there were the French Flying Corps planes that patrolled almost constantly over the city day and night. The army trucks, and small tanks that rumbled through the suburbs day after day. The lorries filled with solemn eyed French troops going up to battle stations. And at night ... the black out. No lights on the streets save the tiny blue flashlights that the people carried. At first it made you think of a crazy kind of fairyland. Then the faint *crump-crump* of a distant anti-aircraft battery going into action, and the long shafts of brilliant light stabbing the black skies, would remind you that France was at war, and that danger might come to Paris, though as yet it had not even come close. But....

At that moment the musical chimes of the French alarm clock cut into his thoughts. He glanced at the clock and saw that it was exactly fifteen minutes of seven. He glanced at the calendar, too, and it told him that the date was May 10th, 1940.

May Tenth! In a flash the elusive bit of memory came back to him. He let out a whoop of joy and flung back the covers and leaped out of bed. May Tenth, of course! Gee, to think that he had actually forgotten. Why, today was doubly important, and how! For one thing, he was now exactly seventeen years old. For the other, that swell French officer, Lieutenant Defoe, of the 157th Infantry Regiment, was going to take Dad and himself on a personally conducted tour of the famous Maginot Line! The Lieutenant had said he would come by the hotel at seven thirty sharp. That's why he had put the clock so close to his bed! To make sure he would hear the alarm, in case his dad in the next room over-slept. Heck, yes! Seventeen years old, and a trip to the Maginot Line!

He danced a jig across the room to the tall mirror that reached from the floor to the ceiling and took the stance of a fighter coming out of his corner for the knock-out round. For a couple of minutes he shadow boxed the reflection in the glass, then whipped over a crushing, finishing right and danced back.

"Boy oh boy, do I feel good!" he cried happily and tore off his pajamas. "Bring on your Joe Louis. Hot diggity, the Maginot Line. Me! Oh boy!"

In almost less time than it takes to tell about it he was bathed and fully dressed and ready to go. He started for the door leading into his father's room but checked himself as he saw the camera on the bureau. He took a step toward it, then snapped his fingers as he remembered Lieutenant Defoe had said that the Maginot Line was one place where even the President of France could not take a camera. For a second he was tempted to take one anyway, but sober judgment quickly squelched that idea. He knew that Lieutenant Defoe had gone to a lot of trouble to get permission for him and his father to visit that great string of fortresses, and it would be pretty cheap to do anything that would get the Lieutenant in wrong.

So he left the camera where it was, caught up his hat, and went over to the connecting door and knocked loudly.

"Rise and shine in there, Mister!" he called out. "Big doings today, remember? Are you up, Dad?"

There was no sound save the echo of his own voice. He knocked again and shouted, "Hey, Dad!" but there was still no sound from the room beyond. He hesitated a moment, then grasped the knob and pushed the door open.

"Hey, Dad, get...!"

An empty room greeted his amazed gaze. The bed hadn't been slept in. As a matter of fact there was not a single sign that the room had been occupied. There were no clothes in the closet, no toilet articles and stuff on the dresser, and not even any traveling bags. The sudden shock made his heart contract slightly, and for a long moment he could do nothing but stare wide eyed at the vacant room.

"Can I be dreaming?" he heard his own voice murmur. "This is Dad's room. I said good night to him here last night. But, there's no one here. Dad's gone, for cat's sake. *Hey, Dad!*"

All that he got for his extra loud shout was a muffled voice protesting violently in French, and an angry pounding on the floor of the room above.

He closed his Dad's door and went down the stairs three at a time and straight across the lobby floor to the desk.

"Have you seen my Father?" he asked the girlish looking man at the desk.

The girlish looking man didn't hear. He was talking on the telephone. Talking a blue streak with his hands as well as his mouth. In fact, in order to make full use of both his hands the clerk had dropped the receiver and was giving all of his attention to the mouth piece. He looked like he was trying to do the Australian Crawl right into it and down the wire to whoever was at the other end of the line.

Dave grinned and stood watching the clerk. The words came out like a string of machine gun bullets. Much, much too fast for Dave to line them up in a sentence that made sense. He caught a word here and there, however, and presently the grin faded from his face. He heard the name, *Holland*, and *Belgium*. He heard *Nazi cows*. He heard *Maginot Line*, and *Siegfried Line*. And a whole lot of the girlish looking clerk's personal opinions of Hitler, and Goering, and Hess, and Goebbels, and everybody else in Nazi Germany.

He did not hear a lot, but he heard enough, and his eyes widened, and his heart began to thump against his ribs in wild excitement. He banged on the desk and shouted at the clerk, but he might just as well have shouted at the moon. The clerk was far, far too busy trying to swim down the telephone cord.

Dave started to yell even louder but at that moment a hand took hold of his arm and swung him around. He found himself staring into the flushed, good looking face of Lieutenant Defoe. The French officer was breathing hard and there was a strange look in his eyes that checked the happy greeting on Dave's lips.

"Hey, what's wrong, Lieutenant?" he asked instead. "That clerk acts like he's going nuts. And, say, Dad isn't in his room. Not even any of his things."

"I know, *mon Capitaine*," Lieutenant Defoe said and held onto his arm. "Come. First we shall have some breakfast, and then I will explain all."

The fact that Defoe was there, and that the French officer had called him by the kidding title of My Captain soothed the tiny worry that was beginning to grow inside Dave.

"Okay, Lieutenant, I am starved at that," he said as the officer led the way to the breakfast room. "But, that clerk. He was shouting something about the Germans in Holland and Belgium, and.... Hey, my gosh! Has Hitler invaded the Lowlands?"

"Early this morning," Defoe said gravely. "Another of his promises broken, but we expected it, of course. Yes, *mon Capitaine*, now France will truly go to war. Here, sit there. Let me order. They are perhaps excited a little this morning, and I will get better results."

Dave waited until the French officer had ordered for them both and put the fear of the devil in the lumbering and thoroughly flustered waitress. Then he leaned forward on the table.

"What about Dad, Lieutenant?" he asked. "Is anything wrong? I mean, is he all right?"

The French officer nodded and wiped beads of sweat from his face with a huge colored handkerchief. It was then Dave saw how tired and weary the man looked. His eyes were drawn and haggard. His funny little mustache seemed even to droop from fatigue. Despite his natty uniform, and the two rows of shiny medals, the Lieutenant looked as though he had not slept for days.

"Yes, your father is well, and safe," Defoe finally said through a mouthful of hard roll. "He is in England."

Dave spilled some of the water he was drinking.

"England?" he gasped. "Dad is in England?"

"In London," Defoe said and crammed more roll into his mouth. "It was all very sudden. Be patient, *mon Capitaine*, and I shall try to explain. First, a thousand pardons for not arriving sooner, but I was delayed at the War Ministry. And there was not one of those cursed taxis we have in Paris, so I was forced to run all the way. You were surprised and alarmed to find your father gone, eh?"

"I was knocked for a loop," Dave said with a grin. "But, look, tell me. Why in thunder did Dad go to London? Because of the German invasion into Holland and Belgium?"

"No," Defoe said. "Some business with your American Ambassador there. What, I do not know. We were in the lounge having a good night glass of wine just after you had gone to bed. A wireless message arrived. Your father said that he had to leave for London at once. An Embassy car took him to Calais where he could embark on a destroyer. He said that he would be gone for three days. You were asleep and he did not wish to wake you. He asked me to take his room, and to be your companion until he returned. He said he would write you from London. He said it was just a quick business trip and nothing for you to worry about."

"Yes, yes," Dave said, trying to keep his voice polite. "But what now?"

Lieutenant Defoe gestured expressively with a butter knife in one hand and a piece of roll in the other.

"Now, everything is changed, *mon Capitaine*," he said. "In a few hours you and I shall drive together to Calais. There I shall salute you and bid you farewell. A British destroyer will take you to Dover. And from there to London you shall travel by train. Your father will meet you at the station in London. What you will do then, I do not know. Your father did not honor me with the information."

CHAPTER TWO

Diving Doom

The small but speedy Renault car scooted along the broad dusty French road like a grey-brown bug fleeing for its life. The ride out of Paris had both thrilled Dave and depressed him. It was exciting to streak past the long lines of army cars and troops on the march. It gave him a kick the way the simple showing of Lieutenant Defoe's military papers cleared the way through barrier after barrier thrown up across the road. Those papers were as a magic charm that made officers and men alike spring to attention and salute. And in a way they *were* a magic charm. They had not only been signed by the highest military authorities, but by the President of France, himself.

Yet with all that it made him a little sad to leave Paris. He felt as though he were running away in the face of danger. He had had lots of fun with his Dad and Lieutenant Defoe in Paris. Swell times, and now he was rushing away from the city. Running away because danger might come to Paris. True, he was only obeying his father's instructions, yet he could not rid himself of the feeling that he was running away.

From time to time he glanced at Lieutenant Defoe at the wheel of the car. The laughter and gaiety had gone from the Frenchman's eyes. His face was set and grim. He gripped the wheel tight with his big hands, and every so often he flung an anxious look up into the sun filled blue sky. Each time Dave followed his look but could see nothing. Eventually, the question was forced from his lips.

"What's the matter, Lieutenant?" he asked. "You look worried. You think something's going to happen?"

The French officer shrugged, and for the five hundredth time peered up at the sky.

11

"Something going to happen?" he murmured. "Of course not. My neck, it is a little stiff. It feels better when I move my head, so."

Lieutenant Defoe punctuated his words with a laugh, but that laugh did not ring true in Dave's ears.

"You're looking for German airplanes, aren't you?" he said straight out. "And you are worried, too, about how the army is getting along. I saw you talking with a colonel just before we left. Did you get any news?"

"We are holding the German cows," Lieutenant Defoe said through clenched teeth. "The English and our gallant troops are now pouring into Belgium by the thousands. We will throw the Boche back. Yes, he shall be taught a lesson he will not forget for a long time."

The French officer lifted one hand from the wheel, doubled it into a rock hard fist and shook it savagely at an imaginary foe.

"This time we shall teach them a lesson, once and for all!" he cried. "We...!"

The rest died on his lips. Rather it was changed into a cry of both anger and surprise. At that moment the car had gone spinning around a sharp bend in the road and there directly ahead was a scene that brought both Defoe and Dave bolt upright in the seat. The road was black with men, women, and children. A sea of people, and horses, and cows, and goats, and dogs was sweeping toward them. There were wagons, and carts, and even baby carriages piled high with household goods. And above it all rose a constant unending babble of frightened tongues.

"Good gosh, look at them!" Dave exclaimed.

Lieutenant Defoe didn't say a word. He quickly slipped the car out of gear and braked it to a stop. Then he climbed down onto the road and Dave saw him slide his hand toward his holstered gun. The swarm of men, women, and children advanced relentlessly toward them. Lieutenant Defoe flung up one hand.

"Halt!" he bellowed at the top of his voice. "What is the meaning of this?"

Ten thousand tongues answered his question all in the same voice.

"The Boche!" they screamed. "They have broken through. They have taken everything. They are everywhere. They will slaughter us like cattle, if they catch us. How far to Paris? We are tired. We have walked for hours. Yes, for years!"

"Enough!" Lieutenant Defoe roared. "The Boche will not break through. The soldiers of France will not permit it. You are but frightened fools, all of you. Go back to your homes. I command you to! Go back to your homes where you will be safe. The Boche will not harm you!"

An old, old woman clutching a bundle of clothing laughed wildly and rushed up close to the French officer. She shook a gnarled fist in his face and screamed at the top of her voice.

"Our soldiers? Where are they? I will tell you. They are in retreat. There are too many of the Boche. And they have airplanes, and, tanks, and guns. With my own eyes I have seen them shoot down anybody, and everybody. I ask you, where is our army? And the English, where are they? I will tell you, my Lieutenant, the Boche have killed them, killed them all. Turn this thing around and flee for your lives. That is my advice to you."

"Silence, old woman!" Lieutenant Defoe thundered. "Enough of such talk! Spies have filled you with such lies. That is what they wish to do. To scare you, and frighten you, and to make you leave your homes, and clutter up the roads this way. Listen to me! I...."

The Frenchman roared with all the power of his lungs, but it was even less than a faint cry in the wilderness. The long lines of terror stricken refugees drowned him out. Like a gigantic black wave parted in the middle they swept by on both sides of the car. The Frenchman's face turned beet red with fury. He shouted, and ranted, and raved. But it was all to no avail. His voice and his actions were but a waste of breath and muscle energy. For a little while Dave tried to help him. He tried to reason with the mass of terrified humanity sweeping by the car. He begged, he pleaded, and he threatened, but it was as useless as thundering at the sun to turn off its light. No one paid him any attention. It is doubtful if anybody even heard him. Eventually he sank down on the seat, his voice exhausted and his throat sore.

He looked helplessly at Lieutenant Defoe. The French officer was a picture of misery, and of burning anger. Tears were in his eyes, and he was working his mouth though no sound came off his lips. In time he got back in the car and sank dejectedly behind the wheel.

"I am ashamed of my countrymen!" he shouted at Dave. "I am mortified that you should see this. But this is the curse of war. The people are like chickens when war comes. They do not stop to think or reason. They think of nothing but fleeing for their lives. They ... they are like children. I am ashamed."

The utter sadness and remorse in the officer's voice touched Dave deeply. He reached over and took hold of the Lieutenant's arm and pressed hard.

"That's okay, I understand, Lieutenant," he said. "Forget it. Look, we'll be stuck here forever if we don't do something. Let's try and get off to the side. I'll get out and push them aside, and you keep the car in low gear. Okay, take it easy, Lieutenant."

Some of the anger faded from the Frenchman's eyes and the corners of his mouth tilted in a faint smile.

"At your orders, *mon Capitaine*," he said. "Yes, you get out and warn them away, and I shall drive the car to the side of the road."

Dave returned his smile and slid out of the car. No sooner had his feet touched the road than he felt as though his body had been caught in the roaring torrent of a rampaging river. Like a chip of wood he was picked up and swept along, and it was several seconds before he was able to regain his footing and force his way back and around to the front of the car. There he put out both his hands and started waving the steady stream of babbling refugees to the left and to the right.

It was tedious, heartbreaking effort, and a hundred times he came within an ace of falling flat on the road under the crawling wheels of the Renault. But for his young strong body pushing and shoving this way and that Lieutenant Defoe would not have been able to move the car forward an inch. As it was the car did not travel more than fifty yards in a good half hour. By then Dave was drenched with his own sweat. His hat was gone and his clothes were slowly but surely being torn from his back.

Suddenly he saw Lieutenant Defoe at his shoulder and heard the Frenchman's voice shouting in his ear.

"It is useless, *mon Capitaine*! It is madness. We will not get any place with the car. The town of Beaumont is but a few *kilometres* ahead. There is an army post there. I shall request a military car and a driver. Ah me, I am desolate that this should happen. Here! Watch what you are doing! You! Let go of me, my old one! *Attention!*"

At that moment the French officer had been caught in the river of people. He struggled and he fought but he was relentlessly swept along and away from Dave's clutching hands. In almost the same moment Dave, himself, was caught up by the moving mass. It was either a case of moving along with the stream or stumbling to his hands and knees and being trampled under foot, or being run over by the heavy wheel of an ox cart or wagon. It was absolutely impossible, and an act of sheer suicide, to buck that packed throng.

And so Dave took the only course open to him. He moved along with the stream of refugees and inch by inch worked his way to the edge of the stream and into a clear space. There he paused for breath and strained his eyes for a glimpse of Lieutenant Defoe, but the Frenchman was nowhere to be seen. He had been virtually swallowed up by the stream of humanity moving relentlessly and blindly forward. Dave thought of the troops and the long lines of army cars he and Defoe had passed since leaving Paris, and shuddered at the thought. When the army and the populace met what would happen? Who would give way, or would anybody? In his mind's eye he pictured other French officers like Defoe striving to force the refugees to abandon their mad flight and return home. It was not a pretty picture to imagine. It was not a nice situation to contemplate. Troops with tanks and guns moving forward to meet the enemy but instead meeting thousands and thousands of their own flesh and blood.

"Please, God, put sense in the heads of these poor people!" Dave breathed softly to himself. "Tell them what they should do for the sake of France, and...."

Dave Dawson never finished that prayer. At that moment there came to his ears a new and entirely different sound. At first he could think only of tons of brick sliding down a slanting tin roof. Then suddenly he knew what it was, and in that same instant the rising hysterical scream of the passing throngs echoed his own thought.

"*Les Boches! Les Boches!* Take cover at once!"

Like thousands upon thousands of stampeded cattle the refugees broke ranks and went scattering madly and wildly in all directions. Carts and wagons were left where they had come to a halt on the road with their horses, or oxen, or dogs standing dumb eyed and drooping in their tracks. Dave stayed where he was for an instant, not moving an inch, and his eyes fixed upon the cluster of dots streaking down from the blue sky high overhead. In the twinkling of an eye they ceased to be dots. They became planes! German planes. Heinkels, and Messerschmitt 110's, and Stuka dive bombers. Winged messengers of doom howling down upon the road choked with wagons and carts, and countless numbers of helpless refugees.

Even as Dave saw them the leading ships opened fire. Tongues of jetting red flame spat downward, and the savage yammer of the aerial machine guns echoed above the blood chilling thunder of the engines. Tearing his eyes from that horrible sight Dave glanced back at the road. It was still filled with frantic men, women, and children, and at the spot directly under the diving planes bullets were cutting down human lives as swiftly as a keen edged scythe cuts down wheat.

His feet rooted to the ground, Dave stared in horror. Then suddenly one of the diving Stukas released its deadly bomb. The bomb struck the ground no more than twenty feet from the edge of the road. Red, orange, and yellow flame shot high into the air. A billowing cloud of smoke filled with dirt, and dust, and stones fountained upward. Then a mighty roar akin to the sound of worlds colliding seemed to hammer straight into his face. The next thing he realized he was flat on his back on the ground gasping and panting for air while from every direction came the screams of the wounded and the dying.

The screams seemed to release a hidden spring inside of him and make it possible for him to set himself into action. He scrambled to his feet, stared wild eyed up at the diving planes and shook his fist in white heat anger.

"You'll pay for this!" he shouted. "You'll pay for this if it takes the Allies a thousand years. And I'll do my share in helping them too!"

As the last left his lips he suddenly saw an old woman, almost bowed down by bundles, trying feebly to get away from the road and out from under the roaring armada of diving death. She took a few faltering steps and then stumbled to her knees. One withered hand was stretched out in mute appeal to the others to help her up, but no one paused to give her aid. Stark fear had them all in its grasp and none could be bothered about the misfortunes of the other.

The old woman was only one in thousands and thousands, but Dave had witnessed her sad plight and so his movements were instinctive. He leaped forward and went dashing to her side. With one hand he grabbed her bundles and the other hand he put under her arm.

"I'll help you, Madam," he said. "Just lean on me. I'll get you to a safe place. Don't worry."

He had spoken in English and of course the old woman didn't understand his words. She understood his actions, however, and there was deep gratitude in the lined and tired face she turned toward him.

"*Merci, Monsieur, merci,*" she whispered and started forward leaning heavily on Dave's arm.

And then down out of the blue it came! Dave heard the eerie sound above the general din but of course he didn't see the dropping bomb. He didn't even taken the time to glance upward. He simply acted quickly. He grabbed the old woman about the waist and hauled her to the scanty protection of a standing wagon. There he pushed her down and bent over her so that his body served as partial protection against what he knew was coming.

It came! A terrific crash of sound that seemed to split the very earth wide open. Every bone in Dave's body seemed to turn to jelly. The entire universe became one huge ocean of flashing light and fire. The ground rocked and trembled under his feet. Unseen hands seemed to grab hold of him and lift him straight upward to hover motionless in a cloud of licking tongues of colored flame. Then suddenly all became as dark as the night, and as silent as a tomb, and he knew no more.

Dave Dawson

CHAPTER THREE

Dave Meets Freddy Farmer

When Dave again opened his eyes it was night. He was lying on his back under some trees and staring up through bomb shattered branches at the canopy of glittering and twinkling stars high overhead. For several seconds he remained perfectly still, not moving a muscle. What had happened? Where was he? Why was he out here under some trees in the dark?

Those and countless other questions crowded through his brain. Then, as though somebody had pulled a curtain aside, memory came back to him and he knew all the answers. Of course! A Stuka bomb. It had dropped close. He had been trying to shelter that old woman. Yet, that had been on the road by a cart, and here he was under some trees. How come? Had the exploding bomb blown him under the trees? Was he wounded but still too dazed to feel any pain? Good gosh, it was night now, so he must have been here for hours!

Thought and action became one. He put out his hands and pushed himself up to a sitting position. Almost instantly he regretted the effort. A hundred trip-hammers started going to work on the inside of his head. The night and the stars began to whirl madly about him. He closed his eyes tight, and clenched his teeth until things stopped spinning so fast. That helped the pounding in his head, too. It simmered down to a dull throbbing ache that he could stand without flinching.

For a few moments he sat there on the grass feeling over his body and searching for broken bones or any wounds he might have received. There was nothing broken, however, and his only wound was a nice big goose egg on the left side of his head. Thankful for the miracle wrought, he got slowly to his feet, braved a hand against a tree trunk and peered about him in the darkness.

It was then one more little surprise came to him. He was in a field and as far as he could tell there wasn't a road any place. No unending stream of refugees, no wagons, no carts, and no road. It was as though he had dropped down into the very middle of nowhere. Completely puzzled by the strangeness of his surroundings, he glanced at the sky, found the North Star and started walking northward. Way off in the distance there was a faint rumbling, like thunder far far away, but he knew at once it was the roar of heavy guns. If he needed any proof he had only to stare toward the northeast. There the faint glow of flames made a horizon line between the night sky and the earth.

"But where *am* I?" he asked himself aloud. "I couldn't have just been blown away. I haven't even got a sprained ankle. Gosh! I wonder where the Lieutenant is? And those poor refugees. I sure hope French planes caught those Germans and gave them some of their own medicine. And...."

He choked off the rest and started running. In the distance off to his left he had suddenly seen a pair of moving lights. One look told him that it must be some kind of a car on a road. He would stop it and at least find out where he was. Perhaps he might even get a ride back to Paris. He would be crazy to try and reach Calais, now. The best thing for him to do was to get back to Paris as fast as he could and send word to his father.

"But how can I?" he gasped as sudden truth dawned on him. "I don't even know where Dad's staying in London. He was to meet me at the station. I didn't bother to ask Lieutenant Defoe where Dad was staying!"

The seriousness of his plight added wings to his feet. He raced at top speed toward the pair of moving dim lights. And with every step he took, fear that he would not get to the road in time mounted in his breast. But he had been the star half miler on the Boston Latin High School track team, and finally he reached the edge of the road a good fifty or sixty yards in front of the advancing pair of lights. Disregarding the danger of being run down in the dark he stepped to the center of the road and waved both his arms and shouted at the top of his voice. The sound of the car's engine died down, brakes complained, and the car came to a halt.

"I say there, what's up?" shouted a voice from behind the lights. "I jolly well came close to running you down, you know. Just spotted you in the nick of time."

Dave gulped with relief at the sound of an English speaking voice. He trotted toward the lights and then around them to the driver's seat. It was then he saw that the car was an ambulance. It was a nice brand new one, and only a little dusty. Painted under the red cross on the side were the words ... British Volunteer Ambulance Service.

"I say, do you speak English?" the driver asked as Dave came close.

Dave looked at him. The driver wasn't in uniform. He wore civilian clothes, and he was about Dave's age. Perhaps a few months younger. In the faint glow of the dashboard light his face held a sort of cherubic expression. He wore no hat and sandy hair fell down over his forehead. His eyes were clear blue, and he had nice strong looking teeth. One look and Dave knew instantly that he could like this friendly English boy a lot.

"You bet I speak English," he said. "I'm an American. My name is Dave Dawson."

"Mine's Freddy Farmer," said the English boy. "I'm very glad to meet you, America, but what in the world are you doing here? Good grief, look at your clothes! Did a bomb fall on you?"

"One came mighty close," Dave said with a grin. "I just came to a few minutes ago, and saw your lights. I'm trying to get back to Paris. Is it far?"

"Paris?" young Freddy Farmer exclaimed. "Why, it's over a hundred miles back. This is a part of Belgium. Didn't you know that? What happened anyway? You say you were bombed? A nasty business, bombing."

For a moment or so Dave was too surprised to speak. This was Belgium? But it couldn't be! Freddy Farmer must be wrong. He was sure Defoe and he had not been seventy mile from Paris when they'd met those refugees. Belgium? Good gosh! Did that exploding bomb blow him over thirty miles away? But that was crazy.

"Come, get in and ride with me," the English lad broke into his thoughts. "I can't take you back to Paris but Courtrai is just up ahead. That's where I'm delivering this ambulance. Perhaps you can get something there to take you back to Paris. Right you are, America. Now, tell me all about it."

As gears were shifted and the car moved forward Dave told of his thrilling experiences since leaving Paris that morning. Young Freddy Farmer didn't interrupt, but every now and then he took his eyes off the road ahead to look at Dave in frank admiration.

"Say, you did have a bit of a go, didn't you?" Freddy Farmer said when Dave had finished. "That was mighty decent of you to try and help that old woman. I hope she got through, all right. We heard that the Germans were shooting and bombing the refugees. A very nasty business, but that's the way Hitler wages war."

"I hope he gets a good licking!" Dave exclaimed. "Those poor people didn't have a chance. They were helpless. I don't see how he thinks he can win the war that way."

"Hitler won't win the war," the English boy said quietly. "He may have us on the run for a bit, but in the end we'll win. Just like we did the last time. That's part of his plan, shooting civilians on the road. I heard a major and a colonel talking about it. You see, if his airplanes can get the civilians to leave their homes and clog up the roads, why then our troops have a hard time passing through. I saw some of that sort of thing myself, today. It was awful, I can tell you. I couldn't make any more than five miles in six hours. And it was all I could do to stop them from taking my ambulance and using it for a bus. I wouldn't let them, though."

Dave looked sidewise and saw how tired the English lad was. His cheeks were slightly pale from fatigue, and his eyelids were heavy. Dave reached out and touched the wheel.

"I've just had a pretty good sleep," he said with a laugh, "and you look pretty much all in, Freddy. Want me to take the wheel for a spell? You can tell me which way to go."

The English boy turned his head and smiled at him, and somehow both suddenly knew that a deep friendship between them had been cemented.

"Thanks, awfully much, Dave," Freddy Farmer said, "but I'm not really tired at all. Besides, there isn't far to go now. Only a few more miles, I fancy. It's nice of you to ask, though."

"It'll still be okay if you change your mind," Dave said. "Have you been driving an ambulance long? Do you go out and help pick up the wounded, and stuff? I guess you've seen a lot of battles, haven't you?"

"Oh, No, I'm not really an ambulance driver, Dave. You have to be eighteen to get in this volunteer service, and I won't be seventeen until next month. You see, I've been going to school just outside Paris and my family decided I'd better come home to England. Well, yesterday several of these ambulances arrived at the Paris headquarters of the Service. They had been shipped clear to Paris through a mistake. The French do funny things sometimes, you know. Anyway, they were needed in Belgium and there were no regular drivers in Paris. Not enough, anyway. I thought it would be good fun to drive one and then carry on to the Channel and on home to England. We left Paris at midnight last night, and soon lost track of each other. It's been fun, though. I'll be sorry to have the trip end."

"Jeepers, you've been driving since midnight?" Dave exclaimed. "You sure can take it, Freddy, and how!"

"Take it?" the English boy murmured with a puzzled frown. "I don't think I know what you mean."

Dave laughed. "That's American slang, Freddy," he said. "It means that you've got a lot of courage, and stuff. It means that you're okay."

"Thanks, Dave," Freddy Farmer said. "But it really doesn't take any courage. I'm very glad to do my bit, if it helps the troops any. We've got to beat the Germans, you know. And we jolly well will, I can tell you!"

The two boys lapsed into silence and for the next two or three miles neither of them spoke. During that time Dave stared at the dim red glow of burning buildings in the distance and thought his thoughts about the war that had apparently begun in earnest. He was an American and America was neutral, of course. Yet after what he'd seen this day he was filled with a burning desire to do something to help beat back Hitler and defeat him. He knew that there had been a lot of boys his age who had taken part in the last World War. He was big for his age, too, and strong as an ox. He decided that when he got to London and found his father he would ask Dad if there wasn't something he could do to help. Nothing else seemed important, now. The important thing was to help stop all this business that was taking place in Europe.

At that moment Freddy Farmer suddenly slipped the car out of gear and braked it to a stop.

"Yes, Freddy?"

"I'm afraid I've got us into a bit of a mess, Dave," he said. "To be truthful, we are lost. I really haven't the faintest where we are. You must think me a fine mug for this. I'm frightfully sorry, really."

"Wait a minute!" Dave cried out. "Here comes a car. It sounds like a truck. Gee, what a racket!"

A pair of headlights was rapidly approaching along the road that led off to the right. They bounced up and down because of the uneven surface, and the banging noise of the engine made Dave think of a threshing machine. On impulse he and Freddy Farmer moved out into the glow of the ambulance's lights and began waving their arms. The truck or car, or whatever it was, bore down upon them and finally came to a halt with the grinding and clashing of gears.

"Come on, Dave, we'll find out, now!" Freddy said and trotted into the twin beams of light.

Dave dropped into step at his side, and they had traveled but a few yards when a harsh voice suddenly stopped them in their tracks.

"Halt!"

The two boys stood motionless, their eyes blinking into the light. Dave heard Freddy Farmer catch his breath in a sharp gasp. He suddenly realized that for some unknown reason his own heart was pounding furiously, and there was a peculiar dryness in his throat. At that moment he heard hobnailed boots strike the surface of the road. The figure of a soldier came into the light. On his head was a bucket shaped helmet, and in his hands was a wicked looking portable machine gun. He moved forward in a cautious way, and then Dave was able to see his uniform. His heart seemed to turn to ice in his chest, and his hands suddenly felt very cold and damp.

He was looking straight at a German soldier!

CHAPTER FOUR

Prisoners of War!

"Good Grief, a German!"

Freddy Farmer's whispered exclamation served to jerk Dave out of his stunned trance. He blinked and swallowed hard and tried to stop the pounding of his heart.

"Hey, there, we're lost!" he suddenly called out. "Where are we anyway?"

The advancing German soldier pulled up short and stopped. He stuck his head forward and stared hard. There was a sharp exclamation behind him and then a second figure came into the light. The second figure was a German infantry officer. He kept one hand on his holstered Luger automatic and came up to Dave and Freddy.

"You are English?" he asked in a heavy nasal voice. "What are you doing here? Ah, an ambulance, eh? So, you are trying to sneak back through our advanced lines? It is good that I have found you just in time. Keep your hands up, both of you! I will see if you have guns, yes!"

"We're not armed, Captain!" Dave exclaimed. "We're not soldiers. We're just lost."

"I am not a captain, I am a lieutenant!" the German snapped and searched Dave for a gun. "You will address me as such. Not soldiers, you tell me? Then, why this ambulance? And why are you here?"

"As you were just told," Freddy Farmer spoke up in a calm voice, "because we are lost. Now, if you will be good enough to tell us the way to Courtrai we will be off."

The German officer snapped his head around.

"Ah, so *you* are English, yes?" he demanded.

"And proud of it!" Freddy said stiffly. "And this chap, if you must know, is an American friend of mine. Now, will you tell us the way to Courtrai?"

The German said nothing for a moment or two. There was a look of disappointment on his sharp featured face. It was as though he was very sad he had not found a pistol or an automatic on either of them. He moved back a step and stood straddle legged with his bunched fists resting on his hips.

"American and English?" he finally muttered. "This is all very strange, very unusual. You say you don't know where you are?"

"That's right, Lieutenant," Dave said and choked back a hot retort. "Where are we anyway? And what are you doing here? My gosh! Is this Germany?"

The German smiled and showed ugly teeth.

"It is now," he said. "But that is all you need to know. I think you have lied to me. Yes, I am sure of it. I will take you to the *Kommandant*. He will get you to talk, I'm sure. *Himmel!* Our enemies send out little boys to spy on us! The grown men must be too afraid. But, you cannot fool us with your tricks!"

"Tricks, nothing!" Dave blurted out in a burst of anger. "We told you the truth. I was on my way to join my father in London...."

"Don't waste your breath, Dave," Freddy Farmer said quietly. "I'm sure he wouldn't understand, anyway."

"Silence, you Englisher!" the German snarled and whirled on the boy. "You will make no slurs at a German officer. Come! We will go to see the *Kommandant* at once!"

"We'd better do as he orders, Freddy," Dave said swiftly. "After we've told our story to his commanding officer they'll let us go. They can't keep us very long. If they do, I'll appeal to the nearest American Consul. He'll straighten things out for us."

"So?" the German muttered and gave Dave a piercing look. "Well, we shall see. If you are spies it will go very hard with you, yes. Now, march back to the car in front of me."

The officer half turned his head and snapped something at the soldier who had been standing in back of him. The soldier immediately sprang into action. He hurried past and climbed into the front seat of the ambulance. Dave impulsively took hold of Freddy's arm again.

"Don't worry, Freddy!" he whispered. "Everything, will come out all right. You wait and see. Don't let these fellows even guess that we're worried."

"What's that?" the German suddenly thundered. "What's that you are saying to him?"

The officer had half drawn his Luger and the movement chilled Dave's heart. He forced himself, though, to look the German straight in the eye.

"I was simply telling him the American Consul would fix things up for us," he said evenly.

The German snorted.

"Perhaps," he growled. "We shall see."

Walking straight with their heads up and their shoulders back, the two boys permitted themselves to be herded back to the car. When they passed beyond the glow of the headlights they were plunged into darkness and for a moment Dave could see nothing. Then his eyes became used to the change and he saw that the car was a combination car and truck. It was actually an armored troop transport. Steel sheets protected the back and the driver's seat, and instead of heavy duty tires on the rear wheels there were tractor treads instead so that the army vehicle could travel across country and through mud as well as along a paved road.

In the back were some fifteen or twenty German soldiers each armed with a small machine gun and completely fitted out for scouting work. They peered down at Dave and Freddy as the officer motioned them to get into the transport, but none of them spoke. They either did not understand English, or else they were too afraid of the officer to speak. And so Dave and Freddy climbed aboard in silence and sank down on the hard plank that served as a seat. The officer got in beside the driver and growled a short order.

The engine roared up, gears clanked and crashed, and the transport lunged forward. It traveled a few yards and swung off the road and around in the direction from which it had obviously come. That direction was to the east, and that caused Dave to swallow hard and press his knee against Freddy's. The pressure that was returned told him that the English boy had a good hold on himself, and wasn't going to do anything foolish.

Glad of that, Dave stared ahead over the shoulder of the driver at the road. At various points the pavement had been torn up by a bomb or by a shell and the transport's driver was forced to detour around such spots. Presently, wrecked ammunition wagons, and light field artillery pieces were to be seen, strewn along the side of the road. They were all smashed almost beyond recognition, and close by them were the death stilled figures of Belgian soldiers, and refugees who had been unable to escape the swiftly advancing German hordes.

Suddenly the sound of airplane engines lifted Dave's eyes up to the skies. He could not see the planes, they were too high. However the pulsating beat of the engines told him they were Hitler's night bombers out on patrol. Impulsively he clenched his two fists and wished very much he was up there in a swift, deadly pursuit or fighter plane. He had taken flying lessons back home, and had even made his first solo. But he had not been granted his private pilot's license yet because of his age.

"But I'd like to be up there in a Curtis P-Forty!" he spoke aloud. "I bet I could do something, or at least try!"

His words stiffened Freddy Farmer at his side. The English boy leaned close.

"Are you a pilot, Dave?" he whispered. "Do you fly?"

"Some," Dave said. "I've gone solo, anyway. I hope some day to get accepted for the Army Air Corps. I think flying is the best thing yet. There's nothing like it. Hear those planes up there? Boy!"

"They're German," Freddy said. "Heinkel bombers, I think. Or perhaps they are Dorniers, I can't tell by the sound. I'm crazy about flying, too. I joined an aero club back in England. I've got a few hours solo to my credit. When war broke out I tried to enlist in the Royal Air Force, but they found out about my age and it was no go, worse luck. But, some day I'm going to wear R.A.F. wings. At least, I hope and pray so. I...."

"Silence!" the German officer's harsh voice grated against their eardrums once more. "You will not speak!"

"A rum chap, isn't he?" Freddy breathed out the corner of his mouth.

"Sure thinks he's a big shot," Dave breathed.

And then as the transport continued to rumble and roll eastward Nature took charge of things as far as the boys were concerned. Strong and healthy though they were, they had been through a lot since dawn. It had been more than enough to wear down a full grown man. And soon they fell sound asleep.

The rasping and clanging of gears and the shouting of voices in German eventually dragged Dave out of his sound slumber. It was still dark but he could see the first faint light of a new dawn low down in the east. The motorized transport had come to a stop in the center of a small village. Dave could see that here, too, shells and bombs had been at work, but lots of the buildings remained untouched. There were German soldiers in all kinds of uniforms all over the place. A hand was slapped against his shoulder and he looked up to stare into the small bright eyes of the German lieutenant.

"Wake up your friend!" the German snapped, "We are here. Get out, both of you!"

"Where are we?" Dave asked and gently shook Freddy Farmer who was fast asleep on his shoulder. "What town is this, Lieutenant?"

Dave Dawson

The German smiled slyly. Then annoyance flashed through his eyes. He whipped out a hand and took a steel grip on Freddy's shoulder and shook viciously.

"Wake up, Englander!" he barked. "You have had enough sleep for the present. Wake up, I say!"

A smart slap across the cheek emphasized the last. The English lad woke up instantly, and he would have lunged out with a clenched fist if Dave had not caught hold of his arm.

"Take it easy, Freddy!" he exclaimed. "This is the end of the line. Here's where we get off. How do you feel?"

Freddy shook his head and dug knuckles into his sleep filled eyes. That seemed to do the trick. He was fully awake in an instant.

"Oh yes, I remember, now," he said. "Where are we, though? What's this place?"

The German threw back his head and laughed.

"I will tell you," he said and waggled a finger in front of their faces. "This is the Headquarters of the German Army Intelligence in the field. I am taking you before the *Kommandant*. And now we shall learn all about you two. Yes, you will be very wise to answer truthfully all the questions *Herr Kommandant* asks."

With a curt nod to show that he meant what he said the German climbed down onto the street, and then motioned for Dave and Freddy to climb down, too.

"That building, there," he said and pointed. "March! And do not be so foolish as to try and run away. I warn you!"

Dave and Freddy simply shrugged and walked across the street to the doorway of a solidly built stone building. A guard standing in front clicked his heels and held his rifle at salute at the approach of the officer.

"My compliments to *Herr Kommandant*," the officer said sharply. "*Leutnant* Mueller reporting with two prisoners for questioning."

The guard saluted again, then executed a smart about face and went in through the door. Dave caught a flash glimpse of desks, and chairs, and the part of a wall covered by a huge map, before the door was closed in his face. He looked at Freddy and grinned, and then glanced up into the small eyes of the German officer. Those small eyes seemed to bore right back into his brain.

"You will do well to tell the whole truth!" the German said without hardly moving his lips. "Remember that!"

At that moment the door was reopened and the guard was nodding at the lieutenant.

"*Herr Kommandant* will see you at once, *Herr Leutnant*," he said.

"Good!" the officer grunted, and pushed Dave and Freddy in the back. "Inside, at once!"

Dave Dawson

CHAPTER FIVE

In the Enemy's Camp

The first thing Dave saw as the Lieutenant pushed him through the open doorway was a desk bigger than any other desk he had ever seen. It was a good nine feet long and at least five feet wide. It took up almost one whole side of the room and upon it were piled books, official papers, a couple of portable short-wave radio sets, and at least a dozen telephones. And seated at the desk was a huge red faced, bull necked German in the uniform of a staff colonel.

"My prisoners, *Herr Kommandant* Stohl," the Lieutenant said. "*Heil Hitler!*"

The big German Colonel lifted his gaze from some papers in front of him, looked at Dave Dawson and Freddy Farmer and started violently. His eyes widened and his jaw dropped in amazement. He got control of himself almost instantly and whipped his eyes to the Lieutenant's face.

"Is this a joke, *Herr Leutnant?*" he demanded in a booming voice that shook the thick walls of the room. "What is the charge against these two peasant urchins? Look, the clothes of that one, there, are in rags!"

The high ranking officer lifted a finger the size of a banana and jabbed it at Dave. The lieutenant flushed and made gurgling sounds in his throat.

"They are not urchins, not peasants, *Herr Kommandant*," he explained hastily. "This one of the brown hair claims he is an American. And this one of the light hair is an Englisher. I caught them trying to sneak past our advance units with an ambulance. They stated that they were lost, and wanted to know the way to Courtrai. When I caught them they were a good forty miles southeast of that city. I did not believe their stories so I escorted them here at once."

"And the ambulance?" the German asked slowly. "There were wounded soldiers in it, perhaps?"

"No, *Herr Kommandant*," the Lieutenant said with a shake of his head. "There was nothing. It was completely empty. It has never been used. That, also, added to my suspicions of these two. I shall give it a better examination at your orders, sir."

"Do so at once, now," the senior officer said and made a wave of dismissal with one hand.

"At once, *Herr Kommandant*," the Lieutenant said in a magpie voice. "*Heil Hitler!*"

The German Colonel waited until he had left, then focussed his eyes on Dave and Freddy, and smiled faintly.

"And now, boys," he said in a kindly voice, "what is all this about? How did you happen to get so far behind our lines?"

"We told the lieutenant the truth, sir," Freddy Farmer spoke up. "I was lost. It was all my fault. I had no idea where I was. You have no right to hold us as prisoners. We have done nothing except get lost, and it was all my fault."

The German's smile broadened and his shoulders shook.

"So, I have no right, eh?" he chuckled. "You are not in your England now, my boy. But suppose you tell me all about it?"

"Very well, sir," Freddy said in a quiet dignified voice. "And you can take my word for its being the truth, too."

The English youth paused a moment and then told the story of leaving the Paris headquarters of the British Volunteer Ambulance Service, becoming separated from the others, and after many hours picking up Dave Dawson.

"And so there you are, sir," he finished up. "A very unfortunate incident, but I've already told you it was my fault."

The big German, shrugged, started to speak but checked himself and swiveled around in his chair to peer at the well marked map that took up most of the wall in back of him. Presently he turned front again and fixed his eyes on Dave.

"And you?" he grunted. "Where were you forced to leave your car? And where is this French Army lieutenant your friend mentioned?"

"I don't know where he is," Dave said. "When the German planes started shooting and bombing those refugees I...."

"One moment!" the Colonel grated harshly. "Our pilots do not shoot or bomb helpless civilians. Those were undoubtedly French planes, or British ones, made to look like German planes. Go on."

Anger rose up in Dave Dawson. He had seen those planes with his own eyes. And he knew enough about foreign planes to know that they were neither French nor British. They were German, and there were no two ways about that. He opened his mouth to hurl the lie back in the German's face, but suddenly thought better of it.

"The spot was about seventy miles north of Paris, I think," he said. "I know that a few minutes before, we had passed through a small village named Roye. And I remember looking at my watch. It was a little after one this afternoon."

"I see," murmured the German, and an odd look seeped into his eyes. "And when you awoke it was night? You saw the ambulance of this English boy's, and he picked you up?"

"That's right, sir," Dave said with a nod.

"And so?" the German said in the same murmuring tone. "So from a little after one this afternoon until your friend picked you up you traveled over thirty miles ... *while unconscious*? You expect me to believe that?"

"I'm not telling a lie!" Dave said hotly. "You can believe what you darn well like. It's still the truth, just the same. I don't know how I got there. Maybe some passing car picked me up, and then dumped me out thinking that I was dead. Maybe somebody took me along to rob me because of my American clothes. They might have thought I had some money, and...."

Dave slopped short at the sudden thought and started searching the pockets of his torn clothes. All he could find was a handkerchief, a broken pencil, and a bent American Lincoln penny that he carried as a lucky piece. Everything else was gone. His wallet, his money, his passport ... everything. He looked at the Colonel in angry triumph.

"That's what happened!" he cried. "Somebody picked me up and robbed me, and then left me in that field under the trees. Good gosh! I'm broke, and I'll need money to get to England. I...."

Dave stopped short again as he saw the smile on the Colonel's face. This time it was a different kind of smile. There was nothing pleasant or fatherly about it. It was a cold, tight lipped smile, and Dave shivered a bit in spite of himself.

"You are not going to England ... yet!" the German said slowly. "There is something very funny about all this, and I mean to find out what it is. Yes, it is rather strange, I think."

"For cat's sake, why?" Dave blurted out. "We simply got lost in the dark, and that's all there is to it!"

"Exactly!" Freddy Farmer spoke up. "It is the truth. We are not even old enough to be soldiers ... unfortunately."

The German officer scowled so that his heavy black brows formed a solid line across the lower part of his forehead.

"Your sharp tongue may get you into more trouble than you think, my little Englisher!" he growled. "You had best take care. Now, we will ask some more questions. You both left Paris this morning, eh? You saw troops and tanks and things on the march?"

"Millions of them!" Freddy Farmer said quickly. "And airplanes, too. I never saw so many soldiers, or so much military equipment."

"So?" the German breathed. "You saw which way they were heading, of course?"

"Naturally," Freddy said. "They were going into Belgium, of course. And not just French troops with tanks and guns, either. There were thousands of British and Canadians. And there were more thousands from Australia and New Zealand, and South Africa. And the sky was filled with R.A.F. and French planes. And...."

The German's booming laughter stopped Freddy. The big man shook like jelly and he was forced to blow his nose before he could speak.

"I must say I admire you, my young Englander," he said. "I suppose now we should become very frightened and order a general retreat at once, eh?"

"You will be forced to, shortly," Freddy said stiffly.

The laughter faded from the German's face and his eyes became brittle and hard.

"Germans never hear such an order, for it is never given!" he snapped. "But, I see you want to treat this all as a little joke, eh?"

"Do you expect us to give away military information?" Dave demanded.

"It would help you a lot, boys," the officer said slyly. "You two want to get to England, don't you?"

"Not that way, we don't!" Dave said, standing up to him. "You'll get no military information out of either of us, even if we had any to give."

"Good for you, Dave!" Freddy said in a low voice. "He can't make dirty traitors out of us."

Heads up and shoulders back the two of them stared defiantly at the officer. He glared back at them for a moment and then as quick as the blink of an eye his big face broke out all smiles.

"Good, good, boys!" he cried. "I like you all the more for refusing. I wouldn't tell anything either if I should happen to be captured. All right, we will speak no more about that. But, I must make out a report. Give me your names, and addresses. I will send word through the Red Cross to your families so they will know where you are."

"But I live in America!" Dave cried. "I'm on a trip with my father. He's in London, as I told you, but I don't know where!"

"What is his name?" the officer said and picked up a pencil. "I will have word sent to the hotel where you stopped in Paris. It will be forwarded to him wherever he is. Well?"

Dave hesitated a moment, then decided there wasn't anything else to be done about it.

"Mr. Richard C. Dawson," he said. "My name is David. Hotel de Ney, Twenty-One Rue Passey, Paris. But, wait! He went to see the American Ambassador in London. You can send word there."

That bit of information seemed to startle the German. He gave Dave a long piercing look, then nodded and scribbled on a piece of paper in front of him. In a minute he glanced up at Freddy.

"And you, Englisher?" he grunted.

"My name is Frederick Covington Farmer," Freddy said. "I live at Sixty-Four Baker Street, London, England. But, see here, sir! You don't really intend to keep us prisoners, do you? I mean, after all, you know!"

The officer laughed and shook his head.

"Keep you prisoners?" he echoed. "Of course not. But I can't very well let you go until I get proof who you are, now can I? In a very short time I shall learn if you've told me the truth. And then, if you have, I will have you put in a car and passed through the Belgian lines. Just as simple as that, see?"

"We have told you the truth," Freddy said grimly.

"You bet we have!" Dave said.

"Then there is nothing for you to worry about," the big German chuckled. "And now, you must be hungry, eh? Well, I shall at once see that you are taken care of and given something to eat."

The German reached out one of his big hands and jabbed a desk button with a thick finger. As though by magic a side door swung open and a German soldier with a Staff Orderly's arm band about his tunic sleeve popped into the room. The officer fired words at him so fast that Dave couldn't catch a single one of them. The orderly saluted and then motioned for Dave and Freddy to walk out ahead of him. When he had closed the door he pointed toward a flight of stairs, and then up. He stopped them on the second landing, pushed open a door and waved them inside. There were two army cots with a blanket for each, a couple of broken chairs, and nothing else. A single window was at the rear of the room and its sill was a good five feet up from the floor. It was thick with dust and cobwebs and looked as if it hadn't been opened in years.

The two boys glanced at the room in dismay. Then the click of the door latch, and the grating sound of a bolt being shot home, spun them both around. Dave leaped for the door and grasped hold of the knob. It turned in his hand, but the door refused to open. He gulped and glanced back at Freddy. The English youth's face had paled a bit, but his eyes were grimly defiant.

Dave Dawson

CHAPTER SIX

They'll Never Beat Us!

"Keep the old chin up, Freddy," said Dave. "They can't do anything to us. They wouldn't dare! Don't let it get you, fellow."

Freddy lifted his face and smiled wryly. There was the faintest suggestion of tears in his eyes.

"I'm not afraid of them!" he said scornfully. "I'm mad at myself. I could kick me all around this room. Through my own stupidity I've gone and lost our boys a perfectly good ambulance. That's what I can't get over. I could chew nails when I think of it falling into the hands of the blasted Germans. I'm just no good, Dave."

Dave laughed and doubled up a fist and put it under the other's chin.

"Hey, none of that!" he cried. "You're my pal, and I don't let people say crazy things about my pals. Gee whiz, you were swell downstairs, Freddy. You talked right up to him when I was all the time quaking in my boots. You bet! Don't worry about that ambulance. Maybe we'll get it back. Heck! Maybe we can figure out some way to steal it back."

Bright hope flickered in the English youth's eyes.

"You think so, Dave?" he whispered. "You think there's a chance we might steal it away from them?"

"We can sure try," Dave replied with a vigorous nod. "You just keep everything under control, and.... Sh-h-h! I think somebody's coming up the stairs. Come on, Freddy! Let's not let them get the idea we're worried at all."

"Right-o!" Freddy whispered back and gave Dave's hand a quick squeeze. "Count on me to hold up my end, Dave!"

Footsteps were now just outside the door. They heard the outside bolt slap back and then the door was pushed open. The German guard stood in the hallway outside. In one hand he carried a battered tray containing food, and tucked under the other arm was a bundle of old clothes. Just behind him stood Colonel Stohl. The big German's face was beaming like a full moon.

"Did you think I had forgotten you, boys?" he boomed and strode into the room. "But of course not. Here is food for you. And take off your clothes and put on these things. I will have what you're wearing mended and cleaned up. So!"

"That's very kind of you, Colonel," Freddy said in a faintly mocking tone. "You're going to be frightfully disappointed, you know."

"Disappointed?" the German officer mumbled and gave him a puzzled look.

"Quite so," Freddy said and started peeling off his dust and dirt caked clothes. "I can assure you you'll find no secret messages or maps sewed into the lining. No matter what you suspect, we really aren't spies, you know."

The German laughed loudly but there was a look in his eye that did not mean laughter to Dave. The Intelligence officer didn't like the idea of a sixteen year old English boy seeing right through him as though he were made of glass.

"Why that's ridiculous!" the Colonel cried. "Of course you aren't spies. I just want to have your clothes cleaned. We Germans take good care of the people we have to protect. You will do well to think of that when you return to your homelands. Now, get into these clean clothes and then eat your food. There, that is better, yes!"

The officer waited until the guard had gathered up the boys' clothes, then he smiled at them and went out the door followed by the guard. Dave and Freddy waited until the bolt was jammed home and then, being half starved, they fell upon the tray of food. The very first mouthful was a delightful surprise to them both. The food was excellent and there was a lot of it. They wolfed it down for a moment or so and then Dave put a restraining hand on Freddy's.

"Wait a minute!" he said in a low voice. "I think this is another part of the trick he thinks he's playing on us."

"What do you mean?" Freddy whispered and stopped eating at once. "Good grief! You think there is something in this food? I once heard a story about the Germans using some kind of a drug that makes a prisoner talk. But I'm starved, Dave!"

"Me, too," Dave nodded. "I don't mean that. I'm sure the food's okay. That's the point. It's swell! I bet the troops don't get this kind of food. Look, Freddy! I've got a hunch he wants to make a hit with us. Feed us up good and then get us to talk about the French and British military units we saw yesterday. You know, they're always after information that will give them a line on what's in front of them."

"Then he is a fool, if he thinks filling my stomach with good food will make me tell him anything!" Freddy snorted in disgust.

"Check and double check for both of us!" Dave agreed. "But here's what I mean. I think we'd be wise not to eat all of this. Let's save some. This bread, at least. We might need it later, and bad."

"You're right, Dave!" Freddy said, realizing instantly what his American friend had in mind. "When we do escape from here we'll certainly need some food to take along. And I think that's what we'll have to do ... escape somehow."

Dave nodded but didn't speak. There was a queer feeling inside of him, and the back of his neck was beginning to tingle a little. That was a sure sign with him that there was trouble ahead. And it had proven to be true more than a couple of times during his young life. No, the German colonel wasn't fooling him at all. Perhaps they puzzled the Intelligence officer, but Dave felt pretty sure he didn't really believe they were spies. Yet, you never could tell. One thing seemed certain, however. The German hoped to pump them for what little they could tell him. He was going to keep them prisoners until he was satisfied. And perhaps he would keep them prisoners even after that. This thing worked two ways. Would the Intelligence officer let them pass safely through the Belgian lines knowing full well they'd tell the authorities what they'd seen on the German side?

No, that wasn't at all likely, and Dave suddenly didn't feel very hungry. He got up and walked over to the rear window. The sill came only to his chin for he was close to six feet tall, so he could see out without any trouble. That is, after he had wiped away some of the dust and cobwebs. What he saw, however, brought no joy to his heart. The window looked out on a tree studded hill that blocked out everything beyond. Another fine day was well on its way and as Dave screwed his head around so that he could look high up into the blue sky he saw cluster after cluster of planes in line and in V formation. And all of them were moving swiftly westward. By straining his ears he could just barely catch the throbbing beat of German engines. Even as their sound came to him he heard louder and more thunderous sounds farther to the west. He did not need two guesses to know that German bombers were once again dropping their loads of death and destruction upon the soldiers and civilians of the countries Adolf Hitler desired to crush under his iron heel.

He turned from the window and stood staring flint eyed at nothing at all. Yesterday he had reached seventeen years of age. But today? Today he somehow felt a dozen years older than that. What he had seen since leaving Paris had added years to his way of thinking, if not to his body. A fierce anger at the injustices wrought had sprung up within him. He wanted to do something about it. What, he did not know. But today there had been born in him a blazing desire to do what he could to spare Europe, and perhaps the whole world, from the bullets and bombs and the tyranny of the Nazi legions.

"What are you thinking of, Dave?"

Freddy's quiet voice at his elbow jerked him from his thought trance. He turned and stared into the clear blue eyes of his new found friend and ally in the face of danger.

"A lot of things, Freddy," he said. "Maybe I'm crazy, but I want nothing better than the chance to do something. A chance to get back at these Germans for what I've seen them do. We may be kids and not old enough to enlist, Freddy, but there must be *something* we can do to help. And, believe me, I sure want to do it. Listen, Freddy, have you any idea where we are? I've never been in Belgium in my life. And I guess this is still Belgium, isn't it?"

"Yes, I could tell from the looks of the buildings, and some of the townsfolk I saw when we arrived," the English youth said. "But what town this is, I haven't the faintest idea. I ... Wait!"

"What's the matter?" Dave asked.

"That map in the colonel's office downstairs!" Freddy whispered excitedly. "Did you see it, and see how it was marked with those little pins and tiny flags?"

"Sure, I saw it," Dave said with a nod. "But I didn't pay much attention to it."

"Nor I," Freddy said. "But I'll bet you something, Dave. This is an Intelligence headquarters, and I'll bet those little pins and flags mark the points of advance by the German forces. Do you see what I mean, Dave? If we could get a good look at that map, and remember some of the things it tells, and then get away from here, why...."

The English youth stopped. He was shaking too much from eager excitement to continue. Dave nodded and gripped him by both arms.

"You're right, Freddy!" he whispered. "It might help a lot if we could tell the Allied commanders where some of the German units are, and what places they seem to be heading for. Let me think. How in heck can we get another look at that map?"

"We could pound on the door," Freddy said, "and tell him we're willing to tell all that we know, if he'll let us go. He'd probably take us down to his office to hear what we have to say."

"Maybe," Dave said with a frown. "But I think it's a little too soon to make him think we're scared and giving in. And, besides, he may not be tricking us. Maybe he really is going to just check on us and then let us go."

"Let us go back and tell what we've seen behind the German lines?" Freddy scoffed. "Not a bit of it, Dave. You must be off your topper!"

"Yeah, I'd thought of that, myself," Dave said sadly. "It's a cinch he's not going to let us go no matter what he thinks about us. Well, the way I see it there's only one thing we can do. We can't try an escape now in broad daylight, so we've got to wait. Let's put on these clothes and catch up on some sleep. The only thing we can do is wait for awhile. Wait to see if he makes any move."

"I hate waiting," Freddy said and started pulling on the old clothes the guard had brought with their breakfast. "But of course you're right, Dave. There's nothing else we can do, right now."

"But plenty later on!" Dave said determinedly and flung himself down on one of the cots. "You wait and see, Freddy. It's a promise!"

Later that afternoon, the Colonel did make the next move. A guard came up to the boys' cell, woke them from a deep sleep and ushered them down to the Colonel's office.

"Sit down, boys," he said and circled around to in back of his huge desk. "I want to have a talk with you."

Dave and Freddy exchanged quick looks, then sat down as ordered.

"Now," the Colonel said and clasped his big hands together on the edge of his desk. "Our Leader is a man of peace. He *loves* peace, and would gladly give his life for peace among nations. You, my little Englisher! Did the Fuehrer declare war on your country, or on France? No! They declared war on him, on Germany. Listen to me! Don't you want peace?"

"Certainly,'" Freddy replied. Then he added, "At the right time."

"No, peace as soon as possible," the German said. "Now is the best time. Before there is more bloodshed. You two boys can help bring this war to an early end. You will be doing a favor to Germany's foes. Now, why not be good boys and tell me the truth? Then everything will be fine."

Neither of the boys said a word. As for Dave, it all sounded as though he were listening to a broken phonograph record. "Tell me the truth.... Tell me the truth.... Tell me the truth!" It was like the title of a song. He sat silent and kept his eyes fixed on the huge map on the wall. He stared at it hard and tried to memorize the dates he could read there, and the names of the towns and cities, and the locations of the pins and flags. One town on the map was well smudged by finger and thumb marks. It was named Estalle and was close to the Belgian-German frontier. He suddenly had a hunch that that was where they were. At Estalle, close to the German frontier, but how far behind the advanced German lines? He thought of the long ride in the motored transport last night and his heart sank down toward his boots.

"Well, for the last time!" the German Colonel suddenly thundered. "Do you tell me the truth?"

"For Heaven's sakes, we already have!" Freddy shouted at him. "We've told you nothing but the truth a dozen times. What must we do to get you to believe us?"

The German didn't answer at once. He slammed both hands down flat on the desk, hoisted his huge bulk forward, and glared at them.

"Very well," he said. "I have tried to be gentle and kind with you, because you are only young boys. But, you refuse my kindness. So, I shall treat you as grown men. I shall have you both *shot*!"

47

CHAPTER SEVEN

Shoot!

If the roof had suddenly fallen down on top of his head Dave Dawson could have not been more astonished or surprised. Shot? He gaped at the German officer half expecting to see the man burst out laughing. Colonel Stohl did not laugh, however. He remained leaning forward over the desk and raking them with eyes that looked like twin cubes of ice.

"Shot?" Dave heard himself speak the word. "You can't shoot us. We haven't done anything! Gee whiz, why do you want to shoot us?"

"Of course we haven't done anything!" Freddy Farmer spoke up loudly. "I think this is all just a bluff!"

"A bluff?" the German snarled. "Do you take me for a fool? I do not bluff at a time like this. Take a look at this that I hold in my hand, so! Ah, you recognize it, eh?"

The officer had suddenly whipped up something off the desk. Dave took a good look and saw that it was a rolled up map.

"It's a map," he said, "but I never saw it before."

"Nor have I," Freddy said stoutly.

"It was found hidden under the seat of the ambulance," the German said in a flat voice that made Dave shiver inwardly. "There are certain marks on it. Numbers and figures written in pencil near the names of towns you passed through before you were caught. So you told me the truth, eh? No, you lied. This map contains information that would be very useful to Germany's enemies. You thought you could protect yourselves by driving an ambulance ... but you can't. But ... and listen to what I say ... you *can* save your lives!"

Dave tried to speak but his tongue was sticking to the roof of his mouth. He felt his knees go weak, and it was all he could do to force himself to stand upright. He had the feeling that this was all a crazy dream, a nightmare. In a few moments he would probably wake up and find himself safe and sound in bed in his room at the Hotel de Ney. He didn't know anything about a map. He'd never even seen it before.

He half turned and looked at Freddy Farmer. The English youth's face was a little paler, but his chin was firm, and his eyes were filled with scornful defiance.

"I haven't any idea what you are talking about, sir," Freddy said to the colonel. "I was not trying to protect myself, or my friend, from anything. I was simply delivering the ambulance to Courtrai. And, for the hundredth time, *I lost my way*!"

The German made a movement with his hand as though brushing the words to one side.

"Enough of that!" he said. "This is a serious business. I am not saying that you collected the information about our advance units I find here on this map. Perhaps you were only taking it to somebody else. Yes, perhaps you did not even know you were being used for such work. Let us say that is the truth. We Germans do not make war with boys, but.... But this information *was found on you*, and that is most serious. Answer the questions I ask you, and I promise that you will not be treated as spies. I also promise you that you will be made comfortable until arrangements can be made to send you home. Now!"

"What are the questions?" Freddy asked.

The stern look fled the German's face, and he smiled.

"Ah, that is better!" he said and spread the map on the desk. "Now, here you have marked a line showing the route you traveled from Paris. Each town you passed through is marked. Those towns are French troop and equipment garrisons. This town here, close to the Belgian border, what did you see there? French troops? British troops? And what was their equipment? Tanks? Big ones, or small ones? Were there motorized anti-aircraft batteries? Were...?"

The German suddenly stopped and looked up from the map.

"You are not listening?" he said softly.

Freddy's face seemed actually to grow thin as Dave looked at him. The English boy licked his lips just once and then put his shoulders back a little more.

"Certainly I'm listening," he said. "But I won't answer a single one of your questions even though you do shoot me!"

Dave felt like throwing his arms about young Farmer and hugging him. Here was the kind of cool, calm courage for which the British were famous the world over. Instead, Dave turned his head and looked at the German.

"We're not saying a thing!" he shouted. "I demand that we be permitted to see the nearest American Consul!"

The German officer ignored Dave's outburst as though he had not spoken. He looked steadily at Freddy for a moment and then sighed heavily and raised both hands in a gesture of despair.

"Very well," he said. "That is all for now. I will give you until tomorrow morning to think it over ... and change your mind. Guard!"

The side door popped open and in popped the guard. Colonel Stohl pointed a finger.

"Take them back," he said, "and stand guard outside the door. If either of them attempts to escape ... *shoot!*"

The Colonel gave them an angry stare and a curt nod, and then busied himself with some papers on the desk. Two minutes later the boys were back in their prison room. The door was closed and bolted, and they could hear the boots of the guard pacing up and down the hallway outside. Freddy sat down on a cot and started to shiver violently. Dave went over to him instantly and put a friendly arm about his shoulders.

"Steady, Freddy!" he whispered. "We'll get out somehow. He was only bluffing. He wouldn't dare shoot us. I'll make him let me see the nearest American Consul. I'll ... I'll make him let me telephone the American Ambassador in Brussels."

"I hope you do for your sake, Dave," Freddy whispered. "But England is at war, and I'm an Englishman. And, Dave ... that map was mine. I used it and marked my route until it got too dark."

Fingers of ice clutched at Dave's heart and pressed hard. He sucked air sharply into his lungs.

"Holy smokes!" he breathed. "Then you did put down all that stuff he was talking about?"

"Oh no, not that!" the English youth said and shook his head vigorously. "I just penciled in the route I had taken until it got too dark. Besides, I lost my pencil when I tried to do it in the glow of the dash light. The rest of the things he must have marked in."

Dave gave a shake of his head and looked puzzled.

"I don't get it!" he murmured. "Why?"

"Don't you see?" Freddy said. "It's really very simple, Dave. They did it to frighten me, to make me answer their questions. They'll hold a military court and use that map as evidence. There'll be an awful row. They'll make one, hoping to scare me into talking. I knew a Jewish boy in England who escaped with his family from the German Gestapo and he told me about the tricks they play to scare you into telling them things. That's what he plans to do with me. But, I won't tell him a thing, not a thing! It's my map all right, but they're not going to frighten me into telling anything that would hurt the Allies. They can't make me!"

"You bet they can't, pal!" Dave said. "And they won't get anything out of me, either."

"I don't think he means any harm toward you, Dave," Freddy said after a long pause. "You just insist on seeing the American Consul and I think he'll let you. When you spoke of your father's trip to London he seemed surprised. You're an American, Dave. You'll be all right."

"But what about you, Freddy?" Dave exclaimed.

"I won't tell them a thing, no matter what they do," the English youth said determinedly. "Never!"

Dave started to speak, checked himself, and stepped back a pace.

"So that's the kind of a pal you are, huh?" he grunted. "You just up and let me down!"

Freddy jerked his head up in blank amazement. Tears were dangerously close to his eyes.

"Let you down, Dave?" he gasped. "But, Dave...!"

"Sure, let me down," Dave snapped at him. "I thought we were pals? I thought we were going to see this through together?"

"But, Dave, you...!"

"Me walk out and leave you behind?" Dave interrupted the English youth's speech. "Quit a pal just because I'm American and he's English? Not a chance. We're sticking together. You can't toss me off like that!"

"But I was only thinking of you, Dave," Freddy protested. "After all I really got you into this, you know."

Dave suddenly stopped acting hurt and angry. He bent down and grinned broadly.

"So what?" he whispered. "So I'll get you *out*. We've got until tomorrow morning to think things over. That's what he said. Well, we're not going to think things, we're going to *do* things. Are you game, Freddy?"

For an answer Freddy put out his hand, and the two clasped hands warmly. The color came back into the English youth's face, and that made Dave feel almost happy.

"Okay, Freddy," he whispered. "I saw something besides airplanes out the window awhile ago. Come over and I'll show you."

For a couple of seconds Dave stood still listening to the footsteps of the guard outside, then he motioned to Freddy and tiptoed over to the window.

"Look out, and down," he breathed in Freddy's ear. "See? The bottom half of this building sticks out. See the roof? It's not more than six feet below this window. And it's not more than ten feet from the edge of the roof to the back yard. Think you could jump it?"

"Easy!" Freddy whispered. "But what about this window, here? It's screwed in."

"Got that all figured, too," Dave said and pulled an army canteen spoon from the pocket of the old clothes he wore. "Swiped this from the breakfast tray," he said. "A hunch made me stick it in my pocket. A spoon makes a swell screw driver sometimes. I found that out once when I was a kid. I used one of my Mother's to open an old chest I found up in the attic. I got a licking for it because I marked up the wood pretty bad. But the spoon did the trick. Now, here's what you do."

Dave paused and slipped the tip of the spoon handle into the groove of the nearest screw head and applied pressure with both hands. He turned the screw a sixteenth of an inch or so and then stopped.

"Hot dog!" he whispered. "I was scared for a minute the darn things would be so rusted with age they wouldn't budge. But, it's okay. Now, you go over to the door and start talking to me. Talk about anything. Sure, let's talk about baseball."

"But I don't know anything about baseball!" Freddy whispered.

"That's swell!" Dave said. "You can ask me questions and I'll give you the answers. But keep an ear open for that guard. If he starts to open the door you ask me, What's a home run? See? That'll give me time to get away from this window. Okay, got it?"

"Yes, I understand," Freddy said and nodded eagerly. "Gee, you're a great friend, Dave!"

"You too, Freddy," Dave said and gave him a push. "Now, get over there and start asking questions. Thank goodness this window is dirty and nobody can see me from outside."

The instant Freddy went over near the door Dave gave his attention to the first screw. The English youth asked question after question and Dave answered them without half thinking. Every second of the time he worked feverishly with the spoon on the screws. There were eight of them and he guessed it was well over an hour before he had seven of them out and the eighth well loosened. That one he let stay partly in so that the window would remain in place. The last thing he did was to cover the screw holes with bits of cobweb so they wouldn't be noticed. Then he walked over to the cot and sat down.

"Okay, that's enough baseball talk!" he said in a loud voice and winked at Freddy. "Gee, how you can ask questions. Well, it looks like we're not going to get anything to eat. So I'm going to try and get some sleep."

Stretching out on the cot Dave pointed at the window and grinned. Then clasping his hands together he put them over his head and shook them like a prize fighter being introduced to the fight fans. Freddy looked puzzled for a moment, then realized what Dave meant, and went through the hand-shaking motions himself.

"Well, I guess I might as well try to get a little sleep, myself," he said loudly and walked to the other cot.

A moment later the two boys listened to the sound of the guard's footsteps outside and looked at the gradually fading light of day outside the dust and cobweb smeared window.

CHAPTER EIGHT

Escape!

Somewhere in the distance a church clock tolled the hour of ten. Dave absently counted the strokes, and then slowly sat up on the army cot. All was pitch dark inside as well as outside. For a couple of minutes he sat perfectly still listening to the various sounds that came to him faintly. He heard the guard outside in the hallway cough and then strike a match. He heard the muffled sounds of hobnailed boots marching along in the street outside, and the clanking sound of tank and scout car tractor treads on the stones. Somewhere in the distance a whistle was blown. He heard the occasional dull boom of heavy guns, or of bombs exploding. And once a flight of planes droned by high up in the night sky.

He held his breath and listened to all those various sounds. He listened to another sound, too, A sound he could feel as well as hear. It was the pounding of his own heart. His chest ached from the pounding, and his throat and mouth were bone dry from the excitement and the suspense. For almost five hours he and Freddy had remained stretched out motionless on the cots. Every second had seemed like a minute, every minute like an hour, and every hour like an eternity. A hundred times it had been all he could do to restrain himself from leaping to his feet and shouting at the top of his voice. Anything to give release to the charged emotion pent up within him.

Four times the guard had opened the door and played the beam of his flashlight on them. The first time Colonel Stohl had been with the guard, for Dave had heard the German officer's voice. He had muttered something about "making them sing a different tune in the morning," and then had gone clumping down the stairs.

Five long hours, and now Dave couldn't stand the waiting any more. Every fiber of his entire being screamed for action. He had waited long enough to make their captors believe they were done in for the night. The guard had taken another look at them only a couple of minutes ago. It would be awhile before he looked in again. It was now, or never. It had to be!

He slipped silently off the cot and crept over to Freddy's cot. He held one hand ready to clap it over the English boy's mouth in case he woke up with a startled yell, and put his lips close to Freddy's ear.

"Freddy, wake up!" he breathed, and shook the youth gently with his other hand.

"I'm awake, Dave," came the whispered reply. "Shall we try it now?"

"Yes," Dave said. "The guard just took another look at us. He won't again for awhile. Have you been asleep?"

"Not a wink, Dave. I couldn't, possibly. Look, Dave. You don't want to change your mind and have a go at it alone? I'll understand. You might get to an American Consul before they caught you. They'll come looking, you know."

"That's out!" Dave hissed. "Pipe down! Take off your shoes. We can't risk making a single sound. That guard may have big ears. Okay, Freddy, let's go!"

Taking hold of the English youth's hand Dave led the way across the room to the window. There he let go, and took out his spoon screw driver and went to work on the one remaining screw. The instant it was out he started to pry out the frame with his fingers. It wouldn't budge. He sucked air into his aching lungs and then worked the end of the spoon into the side crack and used it as a lever. The window still didn't move, and Dave's heart sank as he felt the spoon bending under his hand. He groaned softly.

"The darn thing's stuck!" he whispered. "Swollen tight by the weather, I guess. But.... Gee!"

"What's the matter, Dave?" Freddy asked in a tight whisper.

Dave fumbled for his arm in the darkness and pressed it reassuringly.

"There's a nail, here at the bottom," he said. "I didn't see it, but I can feel it, now. Am I dumb! Hold everything while I bend it down flat. It's a thin one. Then I think the window will slide over it."

Two long minutes later Dave had the nail pressed flat on the base board of the sill. Then he applied pressure with the spoon again, and the window began to move. His face was wet with nervous sweat, and his whole body was trembling. He fought back his rising fear and nervousness and stuck doggedly to his task. Eventually he had worked the window out enough so that he could get his fingers under one corner. After that it was simple. But, as he finally pulled the whole frame clear a corner of it caught on a splintered sliver of the sill. The sliver snapped off with a sound that was as loud as a pistol shot in Dave's ears. He froze stiff, ears straining for sounds of the guard in the hallway.

There was no click of the bolt or rattling of the latch. The sliver of wood snapping had not been heard. Dave slowly released the cramped air from his lungs and gently lowered the window frame down onto the floor and to the side where they would be sure not to hit it when they climbed out the window. Then he took hold of Freddy in the dark.

"You first, because you're shorter, Freddy," he whispered. "I'll make a fireman's step with my hands. Put your foot in it and I'll boost you up. But for Pete's sake, be careful. If we make any sound we're sunk. Okay, give me your foot."

Dave crouched slightly and laced the fingers of his two hands together with the palms facing upward to form a step. Freddy put one stockinged foot on it, and one hand on Dave's shoulder to steady himself.

"Okay," he whispered.

Bracing his feet Dave slowly boosted the English youth up the wall. As soon as Freddy had half his body through the open window he released the pressure of his foot on Dave's locked hands and squirmed the rest of the way up like a snake.

"Get your feet out and then let yourself down by your hands," Dave cautioned. "The roof shouldn't be more than a few inches under your toes. But, watch out. The darn thing slants down a bit, you know."

"I'll make it, all right," Freddy said and twisted around on the sill so that he was hanging on his stomach. "Can you make it alone, though?"

"A cinch!" Dave whispered. "Don't wait for me. Sneak down the roof and drop to the ground. I'll be right behind you. Go ahead, Freddy."

Dave waited until he heard the soft thud of the English boy's feet touching the roof, then he grabbed hold of the sill with his hands and swiftly and silently hoisted his body upward. For a brief instant he sat poised on the sill grinning back into the darkened room. Then he swiveled over and lowered himself down. In almost no time he had cat-crawled down the gently sloping roof to its lip. He pressed flat on his stomach and stuck his head over the edge of the roof. Below him was nothing but a sea of inky darkness. For some crazy reason a twinge of panic shot through him.

"Freddy!" he whispered.

"Here, Dave," came the welcomed reply. "I'm on the ground and to your left. It's all clear down here. The ground's soft. Come on down."

"Here I come!" Dave said, and twisted over and let himself lightly down onto the ground.

No sooner had his feet touched than Freddy had a hand on his arm.

"Well, that's the first part!" the English youth breathed excitedly. "Now, what's the next move?"

"Our shoes," Dave said and pulled the other down onto the ground. "Then we head straight up that hill, there, and keep going north."

"North?" Freddy said in a puzzled whisper. "Why not west toward the Belgian lines? We want to get there as fast as we can. I got a good look at that map, Dave. I think this town, here, is called Estalle. And...."

Freddy cut off his words and both boys froze back against the rear wall of the building as a shaft of yellow light suddenly cut the darkness of night. Dave's heart rose up to clog in his throat as he waited with fear in his heart for the shaft of light to sweep over to reveal them in its glow.

Then suddenly truth dawned and he was almost overcome with an insane, crazy desire to burst out with hysterical laughter. His taut nerves twanged like plucked fiddle strings and his whole body seemed to melt with relief. A light had suddenly been turned on in the building against which they crouched, and the shaft of light had simply been the inside light flooding out through a rear window. When it didn't move where it struck the bottom of the hill slope a dozen yards or so away Dave realized the truth. And so did Freddy a moment later.

"Good grief, that scared me!" the English boy breathed.

"We'll talk later," Dave said. "Right now we're making tracks away from here. Got your shoes on?"

"Yes," Freddy replied. "You lead, Dave. I'll stick right at your heels. Mind your step, though."

"You're telling me!" Dave grunted and started creeping along the rear of the building to the right.

When he reached the corner he stopped and cautiously peered around it. Luck was with him. He had half expected to find himself looking down an alley to the street out in front. But it wasn't an alley. It was just a small court that connected with the next building. A high fence at the front blocked off a view of the street. He couldn't see the street, but the point was that when they started up the hill slope no passing soldiers in the street could see them and give chase if for no other reason than curiosity.

"Stick close, Freddy!" Dave whispered over his shoulder. "First stop is the top of the hill. Here we go!"

Bent over low Dave turned sharp left and went scuttling across some thirty feet of bare ground, and then into the scrub brush that fringed the base of the hill. Hands out in front of him to prevent barging straight into a tree, he started up the slope as fast as caution would permit. By the time he was half way up his breath was coming in sobbing gasps, and his legs felt like two withered sticks that might snap in two at most any second.

He gritted his teeth and called upon every ounce of strength in his strong young body. It was mighty hard going. From the prison room window the hill slope had looked not at all steep, but now climbing up it in the dark, dodging around tree trunks and jutting rocks, it seemed almost to rise right straight up in front of him. Every so often he half twisted around to make sure Freddy was still with him. And each time that was exactly the case. Freddy was right there at his heels, puffing and panting, but sticking like glue.

The English youth's courage and stick-to-itiveness made Dave doggedly refuse to permit himself to rest even for a moment. Freddy wasn't complaining, and if Freddy could take it then he could, too. Freddy might be younger, and a bit shorter, and weigh less, but there was no difference in the quality of his fighting spirit, or of the courage in his heart. And so Dave kept on climbing upward, and upward through the black night until finally ... and it seemed as though a thousand years had passed by ... he finally reached the crest. He staggered along the flat crest for a few yards and then sank wearily down on the soft earth. Freddy dropped down beside him, and for a long time there was no sound between them save the sounds of their labored breathing.

Eventually, Dave pushed himself up to a sitting position, wiped his dripping face on the sleeve of his shirt, and let out a long sigh.

"Gee, am I out of condition for track!" he breathed. "That was plenty tough. I thought we'd never make it. You okay, Freddy?"

The English youth groaned softly as he sat up.

"I guess so," he murmured and sucked in great gulps of cool night air. "But I certainly hope we don't have to do that often. You can't see very much from here, can you? I guess they're not taking chances on showing many lights in case our bombers come over. I'd like very much to see a big bomb drop on that Colonel Stohl, though. He deserves one!"

Dave chuckled and instantly felt much better. Freddy might be dead on his feet, but he still had the old fight.

"Two, one for me," he said and stared down at the town.

In all there were not more than two dozen lights showing, and at least half of them were the shaded lights of army cars and trucks moving along the one main street of the town. If there were others they were blotted out by the trees.

"About that map, Freddy," Dave said presently in a low voice. "I think this is Estalle, myself, but that's not much of a help. I mean, I couldn't figure how far we are from the Belgian lines. I guess it can't be very far, though. They only started the invasion yesterday morning, so they can't have gone very deep into the country."

"I don't agree with that, Dave," Freddy said. "The German blitzkrieg in Poland made as much as eighty and ninety miles in a day. Besides, my father taught me a lot about marking army maps. Of course I don't know what *all* of those markings meant on the Colonel's map, but I'm pretty sure those little yellow pins represented their advanced armored scouting units."

"But good gosh, they were as far west as Brussels and Charleroi!" Dave gasped. "That's miles away. What about the Belgian frontier forts, and the forts of Liege, and such big places? Wouldn't they hold them back?"

"I don't know," Freddy said. "But I suspect the Germans are doing the same thing they did in the Polish campaign. Their light fast mobile units scoot right on past the heavily fortified centers and capture small positions in the rear. Then the bombers and the heavy attack tanks, and such, go at the big forts. It's as I heard my father say shortly after the Polish invasion. You don't have trench warfare any more. It's blitzkrieg nowadays. Lightning attack with small fast units, with the main body moving up behind and concentrating on main points of defense. And don't forget Hitler's air force, Dave. It cleared the way for him in Poland, and in Denmark, and Norway. They're probably doing the same against the Belgians. At least until the British stop them. And we'll jolly well stop them, don't worry."

"Gee, you talk like a regular military expert," Dave said in admiration. "I guess your Dad taught you a lot. War certainly isn't what it used to be, I guess. But, look, there were some blue pins on that map, and beside each one was a date. I saw dates a week and two weeks from now. And there were blue pins all the way across Belgium to the English Channel. I ... Holy smokes! It just struck me. The yellow pins show where the Germans are today, and the blue pins mark places they expect to capture on certain days! Could that be true, do you think?"

"Yes, I do," Freddy said. "I'm pretty sure, Dave, that we've seen something the Allied High Command would give a million pounds to see. Five million, or more! That was an Intelligence map of the whole German plan of invasion, Dave. I'm sure of it!"

"My gosh, then let's get going!" Dave cried, and leaped to his feet. "We've got to get through to Allied High Command, wherever it is. We can't show them the map, but between us we should be able to remember enough about it to help them plenty. We...."

A wild yell from down at the base of the hill, and three pistol shots in rapid succession, cut off Dave's words like a knife. He shot a quick look down the hill and saw a cluster of lights suddenly spring into being. He wasn't sure but he felt pretty certain they were from the building where he and Freddy had been held prisoners.

A second later when more shots and more shouting drifted up to him, he was sure. The guard had probably taken another look, and found out they had escaped. Now the alarm was being given. Bitter anger for wasting time talking flashed through him and was gone. He reached down quickly and pulled Freddy up onto his feet.

"They've discovered our escape!" he cried. "We've got to start moving, and fast. Stick close to me. We'll still head north."

"But why north?" Freddy protested. "We should go west if we want to reach the Belgian outposts as soon as possible, and get them to take us to Allied G.H.Q., Dave!"

"No, north!" Dave said. "They'll guess we're trying to get to the Belgians, you see? So they'll start hunting toward the west, and sending word ahead. If we go north we'll be fooling them for awhile ... I hope. Anyway, it's our best bet. See? There go a couple of their cars racing down the road toward the west. Come on!"

CHAPTER NINE

A Desperate Mission

Dawn was a little over an hour away and Dave Dawson couldn't drag his body forward another step. For hours he and Freddy Farmer had trudged across strange country through the darkness striving to put more and more ground between them and the pursuing Germans. A dozen times they had almost stumbled headlong into roving German mop-up patrols. And once they had crouched for a solid hour in a road ditch while a long line of tanks, and motorized artillery units had rumbled by heading westward.

But now he just couldn't go another step. He didn't care if the whole German Army was right at their heels. He had to stop and rest. There is a limit to the endurance of even the strongest of men, and Dave and Freddy had most certainly proved themselves to be men, not just mere boys, during those hours of mad flight across enemy held ground. Where they were Dave didn't know, nor did he care much right at the moment. The North Star had been his guide all the way, but they had been forced to change their direction in order to skirt bomb blasted villages filled with German troops, and roads clogged with parts of the mighty Nazi war machine, so it was impossible even to guess how far they had traveled, or in what general direction.

Now, though, as he came to the outer edge of some woods and saw the shadowy shapes of barren fields beyond, Dave flung himself down under some bushes and gave his body over to the utter fatigue and weariness which had been trying to drag him down for the last several miles. His throat was dry and craving for water, and his stomach was screaming for some of the bread and the hunk of cheese he and Freddy had so wisely saved from that huge breakfast, and had stuffed inside their shirts before crawling out the window. Yes, food and water would go fine, but later. He was too dead tired now to so much as move a muscle. In a dull sort of way he was conscious of Freddy flopping down beside him, and then a moment later he felt himself slip away into blissful peace.

A soothing warmth on his back eventually woke him up. He started to move but the sudden aches and pains in his body brought a stifled groan to his lips. He stayed where he was for a moment with his face buried in his crossed over arms, soaking up the soothing warmth on his back. Then he rolled over on his back and stared up through the bush branches at the sky. It was another perfect spring day and the sun was well up on high. That realization finally filtered into his tired brain and brought him sitting bolt upright.

"Gee, it must be close to noon!" he heard his own voice whisper. "And we've still got a heck of a ways to go. But where, and in what direction, I wonder?"

He turned and put out his hand to shake Freddy sleeping close beside him. But when he saw the pale drawn face of his friend he let his hand drop back into his lap. He just didn't have the heart to wake up Freddy. The English youth was positively dead to the world, and one look at the completely exhausted expression on Freddy's face told Dave the youth wouldn't be fit to travel even if he were awakened. True, it might be very dangerous for them to remain where they are. German soldiers might stumble about them at 'most any moment. Just the same a strange sense of responsibility took possession of Dave. He was the older of the two, and the stronger. By more or less mutual consent he had become the leader. As the leader he should use his head. And it would *not* be using his head to wake up Freddy and force the poor kid to continue on.

"No, it's best to stick here, at least until dark," he argued with himself. "We're pretty well hidden under these bushes. And ... and, gosh, I just haven't the heart to wake him up!"

His decision made, he put his hand inside his shirt and pulled out the very much crushed half loaf of bread and the hunk of cheese. He ate a little of each and then made himself put the rest back inside his shirt. It helped his stomach a little, but it only served to aggravate his thirst. He'd rather have a glass of water right now than be standing in the middle of Piccadilly Circus, in London, with his father.

He lay back on the ground again and started thinking about his father in an effort to forget his thirst. But after no more than five or six seconds it just wasn't any use. He sat up again and peered around. It was then he saw the farm house and the sheds about half a mile away. Smoke was coming from the farm house chimney, and he could see figures moving about in the yard. Because of the sun in his eyes he couldn't tell if they were German troops or not. Off to the right he suddenly saw a moving cloud of dust. He knew at once it was a car traveling along a road. And presently the car came into view from behind a string of trees. It traveled up to the farm house and came to a stop. Four figures climbed out and hurried into the farm house. A faint hope that had been flowering in Dave died out at once. His straining eyes had made out the bucket shaped helmets and the tight-fitting field-grey uniforms of German officers.

Approaching the farm house was out of the question, now. He had hoped there might just be peasant farmers there, passed by by the Germans. But that obviously wasn't so. The place was alive with Hitler's soldiers. Fighting back his momentary defeat, he got slowly to his feet, took a make-sure look at the sleeping Freddy Farmer, and then crept off into the woods in search of a brook or a small pond.

Remembering his Boy Scout training, he broke branches off bushes every now and then so that he would be sure to find his way back to the sleeping Freddy. As a matter of fact, though, there really wasn't any need of his doing that. At the end of a quarter of a mile the ground sloped down into a shallow valley, and there was a small brook trickling through the middle. With a low cry of joy Dave rushed down to it, flung himself flat, and buried his face in the icy cold water. Never, never in all his life had anything felt so good, so completely satisfying as the coolness of that brook. Cupping his hands he drank until he couldn't hold another drop. Then tearing off part of his shirt sleeve he used it to wash his face and his neck. Finally, feeling almost like a new man, he got up and retraced his steps to his hiding place.

Freddy was awake when he got back, and when the English youth spotted him a look of fear and utter misery was instantly banished by joyful relief.

"Phew, what a fright you gave me!" Freddy choked out. "When I woke up I couldn't remember if we'd come to this spot together, or if we'd lost each other last night. I came jolly close to yelling for you and then I sighted those German blighters over at that farm house. Where have you been, and I wonder where we are?"

"I wish I knew," Dave said. "But I've got some good news, anyway. Go straight back about a quarter of a mile and you'll find a brook. Bet you could do with a nice long drink of water, couldn't you?"

"I should say so!" Freddy cried and sprang to his feet. "My throat feels completely filled up with dust."

"Then hop to it," Dave grinned and pointed. "Straight back. You'll see branches broken off the bushes. I'll wait here and try to figure our next move."

"Be right back," Freddy said and hurried off into the woods.

When the English youth left Dave sat down on the ground and fixed frowning eyes on the farm house. Last night in that prison room his brain had concentrated on but one problem. The problem of getting out of the room. Well, they had done that, and they had put considerable distance behind them. That was all, however. Now, there were more problems to confront, and consider. Number one, was to find out where they were. Number two, was to decide whether or not it was safe yet to start heading west, or to continue north, and number three, was the problem of food. Whether they went north, south, east, or west they had a long road facing them, and their bread and cheese was not going to last forever. They would have to get food some place. And that farm house....

Dave let his thoughts trail off and stop as Freddy came up and sat down beside him. The English boy looked like an entirely different person. His eyes were clear and not heavy with fatigue. There was a lot of color back in his face, and there was a happy and contented smile on his lips.

"I'll remember that brook all the rest of my life," he said. "Gee, nothing ever seemed so good. Well, have you thought up a plan? I fancy, though, we'd better stay here until it's dark. We're bound to be stopped in daylight. That colonel chap has probably radioed a description of us all over the place."

"Gee whiz, you think so?" Dave ejaculated. "Just to catch a couple of fellows like us?"

"I fancy so," Freddy said in a sober adult voice. "He'll be hopping mad that we escaped. And besides pricking his pride it will probably add to his silly ideas about us. Yes, I think the blighter will go to all ends to catch us. So, we'd better keep a watchful eye out even if we are in a hurry. What do you make of that farm house?"

"I've been thinking about it," Dave grunted. "There are Germans there, of course, but there must be food, too. If we could only manage to swipe some food I'd feel a lot better about starting out again. It's going to be a long walk, and it's a cinch we won't be able to do any hitch-hiking with German tanks and armored cars all over the place."

"True," Freddy murmured. "But we might have to walk for days, and days. Then the information we have might not be of any use to the Allied High Command. We've got to get back quickly, Dave, and I'm afraid we can't do that by walking all the way."

"No, I guess not," Dave said unhappily. "But we'd be taking a heck of a chance trying to thumb a ride. Maybe, though, if we moved over close to that road over there, an empty truck or something might come by and we could slip aboard it for a little ways, anyway. Gosh, it seems a hundred years since I left Paris!"

"Two hundred," Freddy said with a sigh. "I certainly never even dreamed that anything like this would ever happen to me."

"Me, too," Dave said and gave a little half shake of his head. "Boy, what I'll have to tell the fellows when I get back home!"

"We're not back home, yet," Freddy said grimly. "Let's talk some more about what we should do."

It was as though Lady Luck or the Good Fairy had been waiting for that exact moment. From up in the sky to the east came the throbbing drone of a German plane. The two boys swiveled around at once, shielded their eyes with their hands and peered upward. The plane was down fairly low and coming straight toward them. A moment of panic seized hold of Dave and he unconsciously grabbed hold of Freddy and pulled them both down under the bushes.

"Gosh!" he exclaimed excitedly. "Maybe they've got planes out looking for us. Don't move a muscle and they won't see us. Gee, it's a biplane, but it's got the swastika marking on the tail. I thought all the German ships were monoplane design."

Freddy didn't answer for a moment. He sat crouched low under the protecting bush branches and squinting his eyes up at the plane.

"That's a German plane, right enough," he said presently. "I recognize it, now. It's an Arado AR-95. It's a two seater, and was built as a torpedo plane. They use it off airplane carriers, but it's a pretty old type. Look, Dave! The pilot has cut his engine. He's gliding down. I say, let's get out of here! The observer in back has probably spotted us!"

"Now, wait!" Dave hissed and shot out a hand to stop Freddy from leaping to his feet and dashing back into the woods. "If they have spotted us we'd not get far before we'd be caught. Besides, I don't think they've seen us. Look! He's going into a gliding turn. Freddy! I'll bet you a million dollars he's going to land in that smooth field over there. Yes, sir, that's what he's going to do!"

"You're right, Dave!" Freddy breathed. "And some of the Germans in that farm house are running out to meet them. But I don't like this, Dave. They may be landing to tell them where we are."

"Nope," Dave said doggedly. "They wouldn't land. They'd either drop a message, or use their radio If they have one. They'd stay up to see which way we headed. Nope. That's some kind of a headquarters over there, Freddy. I bet the plane is bringing them a message."

"I hope you're right," Freddy said in an uncertain voice, as his clear blue eyes clouded with doubt. "There! He's down on the ground, now, and braking to a stop."

"That sure is a sweet looking ship!" Dave breathed softly. "An Arado AR-95, huh? Oh, sure, now I remember seeing pictures of that design. It has a B.M.W. radial engine. (*Bavarian Motor Works*). The Germans used it a lot in training their pilots. It's not so fast as the other war planes, and it's a cinch to fly, they say. *Freddy!*"

Dave almost shouted the name, and his fingers still gripping the English youth's arm bit deep into the flesh.

"Ouch, my arm!" Freddy protested, "What's the matter, Dave? What's up?"

Dave didn't reply. He watched the German plane come to a stop. The pilot and observer jumped down onto the ground and walked toward the group of Germans advancing from the farm house. They met and appeared to talk for a moment or two. Then all of them turned and went back to the farm house. When they passed inside Dave took a quick look over at the Arado with its prop ticking over, then swung around to face Freddy.

"Maybe that solves our problem, Freddy!" he said in a strained whisper. "That plane!"

"The plane?" Freddy echoed with a frown. "What about it? Good grief, you surely don't mean...."

"Why not?" Dave countered. "I made my first solo on a better ship than that. I'll bet you anything you like I can handle it. What do you say, Freddy?"

The English youth gulped and looked most undecided. Dave took the moment of silence to press home his point.

"It's the best bet we could possibly have!" he argued. "Gee, in that ship we could be behind the Allied defenses in no time. I say let's try it, anyway. Gee whiz, Freddy, we might be stuck here for months. There's no telling what we might run into. What do you say? Are you game to try it with me?"

The English youth was already smiling and nodding his head.

"Right you are, Dave, I'm game," he said quietly. "Anything's better than just sitting here. And between us we ought to make a go of it. Right-o, Dave, if you like."

"That's the stuff!" Dave said and slapped him on the back. "They're all inside the farm house now, and if we keep back of that field wall, there, we can get right up close without being seen. When I give you the sign, run like the dickens for the ship. Gee! We've got to make it, Freddy. *We've just got to!*"

The two boys looked at each other, nodded, and then started crawling out from under the bushes on all fours.

CHAPTER TEN

Trapped in War Skies!

Hugging the ground at the extreme end of the field wall, Dave and Freddy stared at the German plane not thirty yards away. The idling propeller filled the air with a purring sound that struck right to their hearts and sent the blood surging through their veins in wild excitement. The feeling of fatigue and body weariness had completely fled them, now. The thrill of the dangerous adventure ahead filled them with a renewed sense of strength, and fired them with grim determination.

Dave slowly rose up onto one knee like a track star on his mark at the starting line. He cast a quick glance back over his shoulder at Freddy, and nodded.

"Now!" he whispered sharply, and went streaking around the end of the field wall.

He reached the plane a dozen steps ahead of the English boy, and practically leaped into the pilot's cockpit forward. No sooner was he seated and snapping the safety belt buckle than Freddy was scrambling into the observer's cockpit.

"I'm in!" he heard the English youth sing out.

Shooting out a foot Dave kicked off the wheel brake release. Then he grabbed hold of the "Dep" wheel control stick with his right hand and reached for the throttle with his left and gingerly eased it forward. The B.M.W. engine instantly started to roar up in a song of power. Dave opened the throttle more and pushed the Dep stick forward to get the tail up as the Arado started forward.

"Hurry up, Dave!" came Freddy's wild yell above the roar of the engine. "They've seen us! They're running out of the house. They're shooting at us with rifles, Dave!"

Freddy could have saved his breath on the last. The sharp bark of rifle fire came plainly to Dave's ears as he hunched forward over the controls. And almost in the same instant he heard the blood chilling whine of nickel-jacketed lead messengers of death streaking past not very high above his head. Impulsively he ducked lower in the pit, and shoved the throttle wide open. The plane was already bouncing over the ground on its wheels, with the tail up, and then added gas fed to the engine caused the ship practically to leap forward like a high strung race horse quitting the barrier.

The sudden burst of speed flung Dave back in the seat, and for one horrible instant his hands were almost torn from the Dep wheel, and his feet yanked free of the rudder pedals. He caught himself in the nick of time, however, swerved the plane clear of a sudden dip in the surface of the field, and then gently hauled the Dep wheel back toward his stomach.

For a long moment the wheels of the plane seemed to cling to the ground. Then they lifted clear and the Arado went nosing up toward the golden washed blue sky. Clamped air burst from Dave's lungs like an exploding shell. He coughed, and shook sweat from his face, and held the ship at the correct angle of climb. The engine in the nose sang such a sweet song of power that for a moment or so it was in tune with the song of wild joy in Dave's heart. The Arado, as he had rightly guessed, was a cinch to handle. It was light as a feather and responded instantly to a touch on the control wheel, or on the rudder pedals.

As the plane climbed upward he twisted around in the seat and looked at Freddy. The English youth was staring down back at the field they had just left. Dave followed his look and saw the twenty or thirty figures garbed in German military uniforms on the field. At least half of them were firing furiously with rifles. The others were shaking their fists, and making angry gestures for the plane to return and land. Dave grinned and shook his head.

"You can just bet we won't come back!" he shouted into the roar of the engine. "We're not *that* crazy!"

Freddy heard him and turned front. The English youth's eyes danced with excitement. He grinned at Dave, and then suddenly seemed to remember the little scene last night after Dave had removed the screws from the window frame. He clasped both hands above his head and shook them vigorously. His lips moved, and Dave just barely heard the words.

"Well done!"

Dave returned the grin and then twisted around front. The dash instruments, of course, were all marked in German, but he knew enough of that language to read them. The altimeter needle was quivering close to the six thousand foot mark. He decided that was high enough and leveled off the climb onto even keel. Then he took a moment or so to glance down at the ground below to try and get his bearings. The first thing he saw was a small village off to his left. One look at it and his heart leaped over in his chest. He saw the hill and the single main street along which trucks and armored cars and motorized units of artillery were passing in a steady, endless stream. The town of Estalle? It seemed to be almost directly under him. The truth made him shiver and lick his lower lip.

If that was Estalle and he was positive it was, he and Freddy couldn't have traveled more than eight or nine miles toward the north during their wild flight last night. Maybe twice that number of miles going around in circles, but certainly not more than ten miles in the direction they wanted to go.

A rap on his shoulder turned him around in the seat. Freddy was pointing at the village of Estalle and pursing his lips in a silent whistle. Dave got the idea and nodded, and wiped make believe sweat from his forehead with his free hand. Then he turned front and glanced at the sun in an effort to decide which direction was due west. Of course there was a compass on the instrument panel but something was obviously wrong with it. The needle was spinning around the balanced card dial.

That fact didn't worry him in the slightest, though. He remembered a tip a First World War flying ace had once given him about finding your direction in Europe when you were lost and your compass was out of whack. It was very simple, too. In the morning, if you could see the sun, all you had to do was keep the sun on your tail and you would be sure to be flying west. And so Dave applied the rudder until the sun was mostly on his tail, and gave his attention to the spread of ground ahead.

What he saw made him suck air sharply into his lungs. Rather, it was a case of what he didn't see. The entire western horizon seemed to be one huge cloud of dirty grey smoke streaked here and there with tongues of livid red and orange and yellow flame. It was as though the whole of Belgium was on fire. Closer to him was a long even-banked river that cut down across the countryside from the northwest to the southeast. He was staring hard at it thinking it was a very peculiar looking river when he suddenly felt Freddy hitting him on the shoulder again.

"That's the famous Prince Albert Canal!" the English youth shouted above the roar of the engine. "It's very strongly fortified. A sort of Belgian Maginot Line. The Germans can't possibly have crossed it, yet. If we can just get by there, Brussels is not very far off. We could land there."

"Germans not crossing it?" Dave yelled and pointed. "Look down there to the left. They're swarming across it like bees. Gee, there must be a million pontoon bridges thrown across that canal. And, gosh, look at all those Stuka dive bombers!"

It was all too true. Hitler's relentlessly advancing forces had smashed the Albert Canal defenses to smoking rubble, thus forcing the Belgian army to retreat to the south side of the Canal. And now as German troops, and their swiftly striking Panzer division were rushing across pontoon bridges to strike more blows at the Belgians, hundreds of Stuka dive bombers were blasting death and destruction into the ranks of the enemy. The sight of it all made Dave's heart turn to ice in his chest. History, terrible History was being written down there by the Albert Canal, and his heart was on fire with an even more blazing desire to do something for the cause of justice and civilization.

But first he had another job to do, and he lifted his gaze and peered at the smoke and flame filled sky ahead. Besides smoke and flame there were countless numbers of planes streaking and darting around in all directions. The air was practically filled with them. There was layer after layer of planes reaching from low down over the battle grounds right up to the sun. And insofar as he could tell at the distance not a single one of them was of Allied design. They were all German.

At that moment Freddy pounded on his shoulder for the third time. And the voice that screamed in his ear rang with fright and alarm.

"More speed, Dave! Look behind us. There's a plane, a Messerschmitt. I think it's chasing us. They might even try to shoot us down. What'll we do, Dave?"

"What'll we do?" Dave echoed and glanced back at the sleek needle shaped plane with its low monoplane wing. "We'll keep on going. They may not try to shoot at us. Once we get on the other side of the Canal, we'll be safe. We'll go down and land."

But even as Dave spoke the words to give good cheer to Freddy his own heart was pounding with fear. The other plane was drawing up on them as an express train overtakes a slow freight. He could see now that it was a Messerschmitt One-Ten. A moment later he saw the gunner-observer in the rear pit shove back his bullet proof glass cockpit hatch and stand up and wave signals with both his arms. Those signals plainly said for them to go down and land at once, but Dave pretended that he hadn't seen. He rammed the palm of his free hand hard against the already wide open throttle, as though if in so doing he might get increased speed out of the plane.

It was no more than a futile gesture, however. In the matter of seconds the Messerschmitt had pulled right up along side them. Dave turned and looked across the air space that separated the two planes. His heart zoomed up his throat so fast it almost bumped up against his back teeth. The German observer was still sending signals to land, but not with his arms and hands, now. He was doing it with the aerial machine gun fixed to the swivel mounting that circled the rim of his cockpit. He was pointing the gun at them and then tilting it down toward the ground as he nodded his helmeted head vigorously.

Dave stared at the gun as though hypnotized. The blood pounded in his temples, and his whole body was on fire one instant and icy cold the next. There was death staring straight at him, and he could hardly force his brain to think. He knew he couldn't just keep on flying. He had to do something or the German would open fire and turn their plane into a blazing inferno. On the other hand, his fighting heart refused to surrender and go back and face the ugly wrath of that Colonel Stohl. For this Messerschmitt had unquestionably been sent out after them at the Colonel's orders. Who knew? Perhaps Colonel Stohl had been the German he had seen climb out of the observer's pit of this very Arado he was now trying to fly to safety behind the Belgian lines. It would have been very easy for the German to phone the nearest air field and have a plane sent out after them.

Tac-a-tac-a-tac-a-tac!

Jetting tongues of flame leaped out from the muzzle of the machine gun in the other plane. The savage yammer sound smashed against Dave's ears even as he saw the wavy trails of tracer smoke cut across in front of the nose of his plane. The yammer of the gun snapped him into action and sent his eyes darting to the cowled nose of the Arado. His heart seemed to cry out when he saw that the plane carried no guns. On impulse he twisted his head around to Freddy's pit, but there, too, disappointment mocked him. The plane was not armed! It was probably just a courier plane used far behind the lines on safe missions only.

As he looked into Freddy's eyes he saw reflected there his own bitter thoughts. They were completely at the mercy of that Messerschmitt flying along wing to wing with them. Unskilled and untrained though they were in aerial combat, it was heartrending not to be able to put up some kind of a battle for their lives.

"It was a good try, Dave!" he heard Freddy call out. "But I guess it's no use, now. The beggars have us on the spike for fair. There's nothing we can do but go down and land, as they want us to."

As though the German in the other plane had actually heard the English youth's words, a second warning burst of shots rattled out to streak across in front of the Arado's nose. Unconsciously Dave nodded his head, and reached out his hand to haul back the throttle. His hand froze in mid air, instead. At that moment he had glanced down at the ground below and ahead. What he saw made fierce, frenzied determination explode in his heart!

They were almost directly over the Albert Canal. He could clearly see the Belgian troops digging in on the south side, wheeling guns into position, and throwing out rear guard action units. Not a mile, not even a half mile from safety. It was too much for Dave. The fighting American spirit of Lexington and Concord flamed up in his chest. He wouldn't do it! He wouldn't give in without a try. He'd fool those Germans in the Messerschmitt One-Ten even if it was the last thing he ever did. Let them try to shoot him down. Just let them try! There were German planes all around, now. And that fact alone was to his advantage. The Messerschmitt gunner would have to take care not to hit one of his own.

"Dave! He means it this time! We've got to turn back!"

He heard Freddy's voice as though it came from a thousand miles away. But he didn't pay the slightest bit of attention. Didn't so much as shake his head. His whole body was cold and numb with fear of what he was about to attempt. But in his brain there was but one thought; one great overwhelming determination of purpose.

He whipped out his hand and eased back the throttle and let the nose drop. At the same time he applied stick and rudder as though he was going to send the plane around and down in a gliding turn that would take them back east. As the plane started to turn he shot a quick side glance at the Messerschmitt. His heart was ready to explode with joy. The German observer had seen the movement of the Arado and wrongly guessed its meaning! The man nodded his head, and let go of his gun and sank down on his seat.

The instant Dave saw the German sink down on the seat he belted the throttle wide open again and shoved the stick forward until the Arado was prop howling down in an almost vertical dive.

"Hold fast!" he shouted at Freddy without turning his head. "They haven't got us yet, and they won't get us if I've got anything to say about it."

Bracing himself against the speed of the dive, and keeping his mouth open so that his eardrums would not snap and perhaps break, he held himself hunched forward over the controls, and fixed both eyes on the flame and smoke smeared ground below. The smoke and flames seemed to leap up toward him at rocket speed. Out of the corner of his eye he caught flash glimpses of Stuka dive bombers cutting through the air at terrific speed. Then from up in back of him he heard the deadly chatter of German aerial machine guns.

He didn't bother to look back to see if the Messerschmitt was on his tail. That would be but a waste of effort. Instead he jammed hard on the left rudder and sent the Arado swerving crazily off to the side. The guns above him continued to hammer and snarl, but he heard no bullets snicking past his ears. He could hear only the thunderous roar of his own B.M.W. engine.

Then suddenly the Prince Albert Canal flashed by under his nose and was gone from view. He was safely across it and right over the Belgian troops! However, it was simply a case of roaring out of one danger zone into another. He completely forgot he was flying a plane with German markings. Naturally, when the Belgian soldiers saw the Swastika painted plane streaking down at them they let go at it with everything they had.

Perhaps it was one of those freak things of war, or perhaps the gods were truly smiling upon Dave Dawson and Freddy Farmer. At any rate not a single Belgian bullet hit the diving Arado, and a moment later Dave hauled the ship out of its mad dive and went streaking along to the rear of the Belgian lines. But before he had traveled more than a couple of miles he once more heard the snarl of aerial machine gun fire behind him. And this time there was more to it than just the sound!

The Arado suddenly bucked and quivered as though it had been smashed by the fist of some huge invisible giant of the skies. The vicious movement of the plane tore Dave's hands from the controls and flung him over so hard he cracked his head on the cockpit rim and saw stars for a brief instant or so. Then as his senses cleared again and he grabbed hold of the controls once more, the engine in the nose coughed and sputtered and shot out a cloud of black smoke ... and died cold.

Realization and action were one for Dave, and so the first thing he did was to yank back the throttle and cut off the ignition. When that was done he shoved the nose down and peered hopefully at the ground no more than five hundred feet below him. A groan of despair rose out of his throat to spill off his lips. He couldn't see a smooth patch of ground down there big enough for a fly to sit down on. True there were lots of fields, but they were pock marked from one end to the other with shell and bomb craters. There was one spot where he might possibly land without crashing too badly. But crash he would. That was certain. There was nothing to do but try it ... and pray!

"A crash coming, Freddy!" he yelled back over his shoulder. "Hold everything, and hang on hard!"

CHAPTER ELEVEN

Fighting Hearts

As Dave glided the crippled Arado down toward the bomb and shell marked field the icy fingers of fear were curled tightly about his heart. He had made one or two forced landings in his short flying career, but they had been like setting down a plane on a gigantic billiard table compared to the task he now faced. If he under-shot the patch of ground he was aiming at he would go plowing straight into a battery of Belgian artillery guns hurling shells across the Albert Canal into the on-rushing German hordes. And if he over-shot the field or swerved too much to the right or left he would go crashing into a maze of shell blasted tree stumps which would tear the plane to shreds and snuff out his life, and Freddy's, as easily as one snuffs out the flame of a candle.

His only hope lay in hitting the field in the center and checking the forward roll of the plane so that when it did slide over and down into one of the bomb craters the crash impact wouldn't be too violent. In his heart he knew that he stood but one chance in a thousand of coming out of the crash uninjured. But there was no other way out, the die had been cast. The engine had been hit and was dead. There was only one way to go, and that was down.

On impulse he jerked his head around and looked back. It seemed as though he had not heard Freddy's voice in a year or more, and sudden panic swept through him. Was Freddy all right? Had he been hit, and was that why he had not spoken? In the brief instant it took to jerk his head around and look back, Dave died a hundred agonizing deaths.

Luck, however, was still riding the cockpits with them. The English youth was still alive, and very much so, too. His lips were drawn back in a tight grin even though his face was white, and there was a sort of glazed, glassy look in his eyes. Being a pilot, himself, Freddy knew exactly what it was all about. He had sense enough not to try any back seat driving in the emergency. He was leaving everything to Dave, and trusting in his friend's judgment. He sat perfectly still in the seat, his arms half raised and ready to throw them across his face when they hit in order to protect himself as much as possible.

Sitting still and showing his faith in Dave by the tight grin on his lips. That realization gave Dave new courage as he turned front again. The ground was just under his wheels, now. He would not under-shoot the field, nor would he over-shoot it either. He had proved his flying skill thus far. The rest was ... was in the lap of the gods!

Ten feet off! Nine feet, eight ... seven ... six! He was hugging the Dep wheel now all the way back against his stomach to bring the nose up just a few more inches before the ship stalled and dropped. His whole body sensed that moment of stalling; that moment when the lift of the wings was absolutely nil. He sensed it now and instantly let go of the stick, buried his head in his arms, and let his whole body go limp.

For two seconds, or perhaps it was for two long years, the Arado seemed to hang motionless in the air. Then suddenly it dropped belly first like a rock. The wheels hit hard and the ship was bounced back up into the air again. It hit again, and bounced again. It hit once more and Dave felt the tail wheel catch on something and send the ship plunging crazily off to the right. He jammed hard on the left rudder to counteract the movement, but it was too late. Fate had placed a huge German bomb crater in the way. The plane slithered over the lip of the crater and charged dizzily downward.

Memory of a wild ride on a Coney Island roller coaster streaked through Dave's brain. And then the plane careened up on its side, and half up on its nose. It swayed there with its tail pointing up at the sky. It twisted twice around and then fell over on its back with a jarring thud. An invisible giant reached out a fist and punched Dave hard on the chest. The air in his lungs whistled out through his mouth, and for horrible seconds colored lights whirled around in his brain, and the entire universe was filled with roaring, crashing thunder.

The spell passed in a moment, and he found himself hanging head downward on his safety harness. His first thought was for Freddy, and he struggled to twist around and look back, but he couldn't make it.

"Freddy!" he yelled in a choking voice. "Are you all right?"

A heart chilling instant of silence greeted his question, and then came Freddy's faint reply.

"Not hurt a bit, Dave! But the blasted safety harness broke, and I'm down here in a beastly puddle of mud. Can you give me a hand?"

Reaction set in and Dave laughed hysterically, and tore at his safety belt buckles. He got them unfastened and grabbed hold of the sides of the cockpit before he went plunging down into the muddy bottom of the bomb crater, himself. He twisted over and landed feet first. It was then he had his first look at Freddy. The English lad was plopped down on the seat of his pants in a good eight inches of mud. And there was mud from the top of his head all the way down. He had obviously landed square on his head but had managed to squirm around and sit up before the sticky yellow ooze suffocated him. Right at the moment he was pawing the stuff off his face so he could see.

Dave plowed around to him and caught him under the armpits, and heaved. Freddy's body coming up out of the mud sounded like somebody pulling a cork from a bottle. Still hanging onto him, Dave ducked under a section of the crumpled wing and hauled and tugged them both up out of the crater on to firm dry ground. Then he dug a handkerchief from his pocket and started wiping off Freddy's face.

"Boy, do you look a sight, Freddy!" he chuckled. Then in a more serious tone, "I'm darn sorry, Freddy. That sure was a rotten landing. I guess I thought I was too good. I should have let you do the flying."

Freddy snorted and squinted at him out of one eye.

"Rotten landing?" he gasped. "Good grief, they can't fly any better than that in the R.A.F., Dave. I thought sure we'd both be killed. And neither of us has so much as a scratch. You couldn't have done it any better, Dave. Honest!"

"Thanks," Dave grinned. "But it was all luck. And I was scared stiff. Thank goodness those Messerschmitt guys were such punk shots. Now, wipe some more off, and we'll...."

Dave cut off the rest short and spun around. A squad of Belgian infantry men was racing across the field toward them. The bayonets on their rifles glistened in the sun, and the cries of wild men were bursting from their lips. The truth hit Dave in the flick of an eye. Those Belgians took them for two members of the Nazi Air Force, and they were racing over to get vengeance for what those Stuka dive bombers had been doing to them. Even as the truth came to Dave one of the running soldiers threw his rifle up to his shoulder and fired. The bullet cut past Dave's face so close he could almost feel its heat. He leaped in front of Freddy who was still wiping his face and flung up both hands.

"Don't shoot, don't shoot!" he yelled in French. "We're not Germans! America! England! Don't shoot! *Vive les Alliés!*"

The Belgian soldiers rushed up to him and leveled their rifles at his stomach. They were a vicious looking lot, but they had been made that way by the fury of war hurled down on them for the last seventy-two hours or more. Their eyes were bloodshot, and their faces were caked with dried blood and dirt. Their beards were sodden messes, and their uniforms were torn and ripped to rags. Their rifles were the only clean thing about them.

One of them with corporal chevrons on his tattered tunic sleeve stepped forward until the tip of his wicked looking bayonet was within an inch of Dave's neck.

"You are Boches!" he shouted and nodded at the wrecked plane. "We saw you dive down on us. Well, you will not dive again. We shall...."

"Wait, wait!" Dave shouted in wild alarm. "I tell you we are not German. He's English, and I'm an American. We have just escaped from Germany. We were prisoners there. We have to get to Allied Headquarters at once. We have valuable information."

The Belgian corporal hesitated and looked puzzled. His men obviously did not believe Dave. They made snarling sounds in their throats and shuffled forward a bit. Dave opened his mouth to explain some more, but Freddy beat him to the punch. The young English boy suddenly stepped forward and a stream of words poured from his thin lips. He had lived many years on the Continent and he knew how to deal with either the French or the Belgians.

"Listen to me, you lugger heads!" he ranted at them. "My friend speaks the truth. We have just escaped from Germany, and we have important information. Take us to your commanding officer at once, do you hear? Do we look like Germans? Of course not! Where are your heads, your brains? Have you not seen us risk our lives trying to reach this side of the lines? Take us to your commanding officer. He may even recommend you for a medal. You hear me? Take us to your commanding officer or I shall make a personal complaint to the Commander in Chief of British Army Staff, General Caldwell. Attention, at once! Take us to your commanding officer, *now!*"

Grins slowly appeared on the faces of the battle wearied Belgian soldiers. The corporal chuckled and lowered his bayonet from Dave's throat.

"The little one spits fire when he speaks," he murmured and nodded his head. "No, I do not believe now that you are Germans. But you had a very lucky escape, my two little ones. We do not feel very pleased today. Nor will we be happy for a long time to come, I am afraid. It looks bad, very bad. Come! I will take you to my Lieutenant."

"It looks bad?" Freddy asked quickly. "Can't you hold them? Aren't the British and the French helping?"

The Belgian corporal shrugged and wiped his tired eyes with a dirt and mud smeared hand.

"It is possible," he grunted. "I do not know. We hear very little except the guns and those cursed bombs. But, there are no British or French here. Only Belgians. And we cannot stop them. We have not the men, or the guns, or the tanks. And planes? Where are all our planes? Look at the sky! It is filled with nothing but Boche planes. Yes, my little one, it looks very bad. But we are not afraid to die. No!"

The soldier shrugged again, then nodded with his head and started trudging back across the field, trailing his rifle as though it weighed a ton instead of a few pounds or so. Freddy and Dave dropped into step with the others and went along. Nobody spoke. Nobody but the bombs and the shells but a few miles away, and rapidly drawing closer. Dave leaned toward Freddy.

"Boy, can you dish out their language!" he breathed. "But I don't blame them. They must have been through something terrible. It's a wonder they didn't shoot and ask questions afterward."

"Yes," Freddy said in a dull voice. "I wonder where the French and the British are? I hope they can get here in time."

Dave didn't attempt to answer the question. He suddenly felt very tired, and old. His strength had been sapped to the limit, and his spirits were staggering under a crushing weight. The picture of those German hordes pouring across the Albert Canal and virtually beating the Belgians right down into the ground was still clear as crystal in his brain. It was like a mighty tidal wave hurtling forward with nothing but a picket fence in the way to stop it.

At the far end of the field the Belgians turned left on a winding narrow dirt road. They went down this for some fifty yards or so, then left the road and entered some woods. In the heart of the woods several companies of Belgian troops were frantically building up machine gun emplacements, stringing out barbwire, and moving light field pieces into place to bear on the winding dirt road. The corporal stopped before a young lieutenant and saluted smartly. Dave and Freddy stopped and waited while the corporal spoke to the officer.

In a moment or so the lieutenant came over and stared at them both out of bleak, dead tired eyes.

"What is all this?" he demanded briskly.

Dave let Freddy do the talking as he had the language down perfect. The young Englishman talked a steady stream for two or three moments, giving a brief account of their movements since the day the Nazi armies broke through into Belgium and the Low Countries. The Belgian officer listened in silence, and when Freddy finished he took a map from his pocket and spread it out on the ground.

"Where were some of those pins and flags you saw on that map?" he asked.

Dave still let Freddy do the talking, and simply watched while the English youth pointed out various points on the map. The Belgian nodded his head from time to time, and presently folded the map and got quickly to his feet.

"I am positive you have seen a map of great importance!" he said. "I will see that you are taken to Belgian G.H.Q. at once. You will tell them all you know, and they will communicate with the Allied High Command. You are very brave boys, you know?"

Freddy flushed and looked uncomfortable.

"We only want to do everything we can to help," he said quietly.

The Lieutenant's tired lips twisted back in a wistful smile as he glanced from Freddy to Dave.

"I would feel very happy if I had a million like you under my command," he murmured. "If only half what you say is true, it is enough. Sergeant!"

A huge bearded non-com putting a machine gun in working order got to his feet and lumbered over. He ran his bloodshot eyes over Freddy and Dave, and then fixed them on his officer.

"My Lieutenant?" he grunted.

"These two, Sergeant," the Lieutenant said with a jerk of his head. "They are to be taken to General Boulard's headquarters at once. You will take one of the light scouting cars and drive them there. That is all."

The big sergeant blinked and looked dubious.

"I will try, of course, my Lieutenant," he said. "But we may meet with difficulty. A runner has arrived only a moment ago at the Fortieth Company. The Boche tanks have cut the road to Namur. They seek to get around in back of us. The Boche planes are also bombing the entire road. It will be difficult but I will attempt it, my Lieutenant."

Dave saw the Belgian officer's face pale under its coating of blood and dirt. The man clenched his fists in a helpless gesture, and something akin to tears of bitter rage glistened in his haggard eyes. At that exact moment the whole world was filled with a terrifying eerie scream. The Belgians fell flat on their faces. The Lieutenant dragged Freddy and Dave down with him, and tried to cover them with his own body.

Dave knew the meaning of that awful sound. He had heard it along that road packed with terror stricken refugees. He had heard it as he dragged an old woman to the flimsy protection of an ox cart. His heart stood still in his chest. The blood ceased to surge through his veins. His lungs became locked with air, and his brain became numb and useless as he waited those terrible few seconds. The diving Stuka's death load hit on the far side of the road. Half of Belgium seemed to fountain up into the sky, and what was left rocked and swayed crazily. Thunderous sound swept over Dave and seemed actually to shove him down into the ground. In a crazy sort of way he wondered if he was dead. Then the next thing he realized the Belgian lieutenant was helping him up onto his feet.

"It is only the direct hits that matter," the officer said in a gentle voice, and smiled.

"That was plenty direct enough for me!" Dave said and gulped.

"Yes, quite!" Freddy breathed and clenched his hands to stop his fingers trembling.

"When they dive several at a time, then it is not pleasant," the Belgian infantry officer said. "But one can only pray. That is the way with war. But, about this trip to General Boulard's headquarters. You heard what the Sergeant said? It may be very dangerous. Perhaps you would care to wait awhile, and rest?"

Something in the officer's tone made Dave jerk his head up.

"Hey, I wasn't *that* scared!" he blurted out. "We're ready to start right now. Okay, Freddy?"

"Of course," the English youth replied instantly. "Let's start at once. The sooner we get there, the better."

"You are good soldiers, and I salute you," the officer murmured. "Very well, then. And all my good wishes. After all, perhaps it is not best to wait here. Soon we shall be very busy, here. Yes, very busy. Sergeant! You have your orders."

The tired Belgian officer clicked his heels and saluted the two boys. They returned the salute and as Dave looked into the Belgian's eyes he saw a look there he would never forget as long as he lived. That officer knew what was coming toward him from the Albert Canal. He knew that he would stay where he was and face it. And he also knew that he would probably never live to see another sunrise. In a few words he had told of all that was in his thoughts. He had simply said, "Soon we shall be very busy, here."

The Belgian's loyalty and great courage stirred Dave to the depths of his soul. He impulsively reached out and grasped the officer's hand and shook it.

"I hope you beat the stuffing out of them. Lieutenant," he said in a rush of words. "Freddy and I will be rooting for you, and how!"

"You bet we will!" the English youth echoed. "I jolly well hope you chase them all the way back to Berlin!"

The Belgian officer made no reply. He smiled at them sadly and saluted again. The boys turned away and followed the big Sergeant through the patch of woods to the far side where a unit of small tanks and scouting cars was parked in under the trees. The Sergeant climbed in behind the wheel of the nearest scouting car and motioned the two youths to get in back. A couple of moments later the engine was doing its work and the Sergeant was skillfully tooling the car across open fields toward the southwest.

For a few moments Dave stared at the frenzied activity of the Belgian troops that were all around them. Inexperienced though he was in military technique, and so forth, he instinctively knew that the brave Belgians were making feverish preparations for a last ditch stand against the Germans. And with the picture of the Albert Canal crossing still fresh in his memory he knew in his heart that all he saw would be just a waste of gallant effort. Those German hordes, protected by their swarms of planes, would go right through as though the Belgians weren't there at all. It actually made his heart hurt to watch them and so he slumped down in the seat of the car, and let his body sway with the bumps, and stared moodily at the back of the driver's neck.

Presently Freddy reached over and placed a hand on his knee and pressed it.

"Chin up, Dave!" he heard Freddy say. "We'll get through all right, you wait and see."

Dave shook his head and sat up a bit and grinned.

"Sure we'll make it," he said. "I'm not worrying about that. I was just thinking."

"About what?" Freddy asked.

"Well, just then I was thinking about that Arado I cracked up," Dave said. "I sure feel rotten about that. I wish I could have brought it down all in one piece."

"Good grief, forget it!" Freddy gasped. "It was wonderful of you to get it down at all. I would have killed us both, for fair. I can tell you, now, that I was very scared when you took off. I didn't know then how well you could fly, but I do, now. You're a little bit of all right, Dave. I mean that, really!"

"You're swell to say that, anyway," Dave grinned. "I'm still sorry, though, I had to go and crack it up. I don't know ... Well, I guess a plane to me is something like what his horse is to a cow puncher. It's ... it's almost something human."

"I know what you mean, Dave."

"Do you, Freddy?" Dave echoed. "Well, that's the way it is. And I'll tell you something, but you'll probably think I'm nuts. I made an awful punk landing when I made my first solo. Cracked up the ship. I busted a wing and wiped the undercarriage right off, and didn't get a scratch. But do you know? I felt so bad about it I busted right out bawling like a kid. My instructor was scared stiff. He thought something awful had happened to me. But when I finally cut it out he was swell about the whole thing. He said it was the normal reaction of a fellow who could really go for flying. It made me feel better anyway. Yeah, I sure feel pretty punk for busting up that Arado, even though it was a German crate."

Freddy started to speak but Dave didn't even hear the first word. The car had bounced out of a field and was being swung onto a road when the landscape on all four sides suddenly blossomed up with spouting geysers of brilliant red flame and towering columns of oily black smoke. Thunderous sound rushed at them and seemed to lift the small scouting car straight up into the air.

"Shrapnel barrage!" the Sergeant screamed and slammed on the brakes. "Take cover under the car at once!"

Dave Dawson

CHAPTER TWELVE

In the Nick of Time

Huddled together like sardines under the car, the Belgian Sergeant and the two boys pressed fingers to their ears while all about them a whole world went mad with shot and shell. Never in all his life had Dave heard such a bellowing roar of crashing sound. For the first few seconds his entire body had been paralyzed with fear, but when he didn't die at once his brain grew kind of numb, and the roaring thunder didn't seem to have so much effect upon him. It wasn't because of a greater courage coming to his rescue. And it wasn't a lack of fear, either. It was simply that in the midst of a furious bombardment the minds of human beings are too stunned by the sound to register any kind of emotion.

And so the three of them just lay there under the car while the German gunners far back expended their wrath in the form of screaming steel, and mountains of flame and rolling thunder. In ten minutes it was all over. The range of the guns was changed and the barrage moved onward to some other objective. Yet neither of the three moved a muscle. It was as though each was waiting for the other to make the first move.

Eventually Dave could stand the suspense no longer. He jerked up his head without thinking and cracked it hard on the underside of the car. He let out a yelp of pain, and the sound of his voice seemed to release whatever was holding Freddy Farmer and the Belgian Sergeant. All three of them crawled out from under the car and got to their feet and looked around. Dave and Freddy gasped aloud. The Belgian Sergeant shrugged indifferently and muttered through his teeth. There just wasn't any road any more. It was completely lost in a vast area of smoking shell holes that seemed to stretch out in all directions as far as the eye could see. Blackened jagged stumps marked what had once been trees. Fields where spring grass had been growing up were now brown acres of piled up dirt and stones. And a spot where Dave had last seen a farm house was as bare as the palm of his hand.

"By the Saints, you two are a lucky charm!" the Sergeant suddenly exploded and bobbed his big head up and down vigorously. "If you could stay by my side always I would come out of this war alive without any trouble at all. By the Saints of Notre Dame, yes! Look at the car. It has not even been scratched! It is a miracle, nothing else!"

It was true! The small scouting car was bathed in dust and dirt but there wasn't so much as a scratch on it. The engine was even idling as smooth as could be. The Belgian Sergeant stared at it almost as though he were staring at a ghost. Then shaking his head and muttering through his big buck teeth, he climbed in behind the wheel.

"Nothing can possibly be as bad as that," he said. "Let us proceed at once while the Good Lady still smiles upon us. Name of all things wonderful, I can hardly believe I am still alive. *En avant, mes enfants!*"

With a sudden contempt for the shell blasted ground, that made Dave and Freddy grin in spite of the harrowing experience through which they had just past, the Sergeant sent the car scooting in and out around the craters with the careless ease of driving along a wide boulevard. In less time than it takes to tell about it he had driven clear out of the barrage area and was skirting around a patch of woods toward another and as yet untouched road. And to show the kind of stuff he was made of the man began singing joyfully at the top of his voice.

For the next half hour the war seemed to fade far away. True there were signs of it on all sides, and above their heads, but a certain feeling of security came to the boys as the Sergeant bumped them along roads and across fields skirting around shell holes, artillery batteries, and reserve troops being rushed up to the Front. Yet somehow all that didn't touch them, now. A few hours ago they had been hiding in enemy territory, two hunted prisoners of war. But now they were well behind the Belgian lines and speeding toward headquarters where they would deliver enemy position information that would be of great value to the Allies. Two youths, sixteen and seventeen, had beaten the Germans at their own game. Instead of revealing information of value to the Germans, they had escaped with German information valuable to the Allies.

Dave leaned his head back and sighed restfully. It sure made a fellow feel good to have been of some help. And it made him feel twice as good to have a pal like Freddy Farmer along with him. Freddy had certainly proved his mettle in the tight corners. And regardless of what he'd said, Freddy probably would have done a better job of flying that Arado, too. At every turn the English youth popped up with a new side to him. He sure was glad Freddy and his ambulance had come along when they had. And, gee, just how long ago was that, anyway? Three days, or three years? It had been plenty long ago anyway.

At that moment Freddy suddenly sat forward and tapped the Sergeant on the shoulder.

"Why are we heading east?" he asked and pointed at the last rays of the setting sun. "If you're trying to get to Namur, you're going in the wrong direction."

"That is so," the Sergeant called back. "But, it is necessary. The Boches have cut the road, and we must go around them. Soon it will be dark. It will not be so hard when it is dark. Do not worry, my little one, we shall get there."

Freddy started to argue but seemed to think better of it. He sank back on the seat scowling thoughtfully at the setting sun. Dave looked at him a moment, and then spoke.

"What gives, Freddy?" he asked. "Do you think the Sergeant doesn't know what he's doing?"

"No, he's probably right," the English youth said. "If the Namur road has been cut by the Germans we've got to go around them, of course. But I've spent several summers in this part of Belgium, and...."

Freddy stopped short and leaned forward once more.

"Why can't we circle around them on the west, Sergeant?" he shouted. "Can't you cut over and take the road leading south from Wavre?"

The Belgian let out a yell of consternation and stopped the car so suddenly he almost pitched the two boys right over the back of the front seat.

"The brain of a cat I have!" he shouted and thumped a big fist against his forehead. "But, of course, of course, my little one! Those bombs and shells! They must have made scrambled eggs out of what I have in my head!"

Taking his foot off the brake the Belgian shifted back into low gear and got the car underway again. At a crossroads some hundred yards ahead he turned sharp right and fed gas to the engine. A moment later a machine gun yammered savagely behind them. Dave twisted around in the seat and saw an armored car bearing German army insignia racing for the turn-off they had taken, but from the opposite direction. There was a machine gun mounted on the car and a helmeted German soldier was striving to get them in his range.

The Belgian Sergeant took one quick glance back over his shoulder and instantly gave the engine all the gas it could take.

"A lucky charm you are indeed!" he shouted and hunched forward over the wheel. "If you had not put sense in my head, and I had not turned off on to this road, we would have run right into them. And that would have been bad, very bad. Name of the Saints, the Lieutenant will reduce me to a corporal when he hears of this!"

Neither Dave nor Freddy bothered to make any comment. To tell the truth they were too busy hanging on tight and trying to stay in the car as it rocketed forward seeming virtually to leap across shell holes in the road. The Sergeant perhaps did not have very many brains but he certainly knew how to handle that small scouting car. He skipped across shell holes, dodged and twisted about trees blown down across it, and roared right through scattered wreckage of bombed supply trucks and the like as though they weren't even there. And all the time the machine gun farther back snarled and yammered out its song of death.

The pursuing Germans had swung on to their road and were now striving desperately to overtake them. Dave stuck his head up to see if they had gained, but before he could see anything Freddy grabbed him around the waist and practically threw him down onto the floor of the car.

"Stay down, Dave!" the English youth shouted above the roar of the little car's powerful engine. "We've ducked enough bullets for one day. Don't be crazy!"

Dave grinned sheepishly and nodded.

"That was dumb!" he said. "You're right, and thanks!"

As the last left his lips a burst of bullets whined low over the car. Dave gulped and ducked his head.

"Thanks, and how!" he yelled. "Boy, those were close. If I'd been looking back they might ... *Hey!*"

At that moment the little car turned sharply to the right and seemed to zoom right up into the air. It came down with a crashing jolt. A shower of bush branches slithered down on the boys and they were tossed around in the back of the car like two peas in a pod. Puffing and panting, they struggled to brace themselves before they were pitched out head over heels. No sooner would they get a firm hold on something than the scout car would careen up on its side and go darting off in another direction, and they would be bounced around again.

For a good ten minutes they tore through the darkening twilight first this way and then that way. Then suddenly the violent jolting ceased abruptly, and the car ran along on an even keel. Covered with bumps and bruises from head to toe, the two boys scrambled up off the floor of the car and flopped down on the seat. The Belgian Sergeant pushed on the brake and brought the car to a halt under the shelter of over-hanging tree branches. He switched the engine off and turned around and smiled at them triumphantly.

"We have lost the Boches!" he announced. "Everything is all right, now. When it gets dark we will continue. You, my little lucky charm, I must thank you for putting sense in my head."

"That's quite, all right," Freddy said and fingered a lump behind his right ear. "That was a fine bit of driving, Sergeant, even though you came close to breaking our necks. Next time, though, please let us know in time."

"You said it!" Dave gasped and nursed a barked shin. "And when you do, I'm going to jump out. Boy, talk about your wild rides!"

The Belgian Sergeant laughed and gestured with his big hands.

"But that was nothing!" he protested, "These little cars, they can go up the side of a cliff. That German thing? Bah! It creeps along like a snail. You should have been with me and the Lieutenant yesterday. Ah, that was a ride! For a whole hour, mind you. And they were shooting at us from all sides. But we got through without a scratch. It was wonderful. You should have been there!"

"I think I'm glad I wasn't," Freddy said, and smiled so the Belgian would not feel hurt. "But what, now? Where are we?"

Before he would reply the Belgian stuck a dirty cigarette between his lips and lighted up.

"We wait for the darkness, and that will not be long," he finally said. Then pointing across the field to the left, he continued, "One mile in that direction and we strike a road that will lead us straight into the Wavre-Namur road. Two hours at the most and we shall be there."

"Unless the Germans have cut it, too," Freddy murmured.

The Belgian looked at him and snorted.

"Impossible!" he said in a decisive voice. "They cannot have advanced that far. Don't worry, *mes enfants*, I will get you to Namur in no time at all. I ... *Sacré!* Those are German tank guns!"

The pounding of guns had suddenly broken out from behind them and to the left. Not the deep booming sound of long range pieces, but the sharp bark of small caliber guns. The sergeant pinched out his cigarette and stuck it in his pocket and slid out of the car. He stood motionless for a moment, head cocked on one side and listening intently to the guns. Dave listened, too, trying to tell if they were coming closer. A strip of woods broke up the sound, and it was impossible for him to tell.

He glanced at the sergeant and was startled to see the worried look on the man's face. Worry and astonishment, as though the Belgian was trying to convince himself that the truth was false. In the fast fading light the lines of his face deepened until it became a face of shadows. Suddenly he muttered something under his breath and pulled a Belgian army pistol from the holster at his side.

"Remain here!" he ordered in a hard voice. "This is most strange, and I must investigate. Those cannot be German guns, but perhaps so. I will go and look, and return at once. Remain here, and wait!"

Without waiting for either of them to say a word, the Belgian glided swiftly away from the car and was almost at once swallowed up in the shadows cast by the trees. Dave looked at Freddy.

"What do you think?" he asked. "If that's Germans coming this way, we're crazy to stick around. Don't you think so?"

"Yes, I do," the English youth said bluntly. "But let's wait a little bit. They may not be, and it wouldn't be quite fair dashing off and leaving the Sergeant to walk back, you know."

"Okay, we'll wait, then," Dave agreed. "Boy, but wasn't that some wild ride! And it sure was lucky you spoke to him when you did. What I mean, you saved us from a tough spot. Hey, what's that?"

The tank guns had gone silent, but the yammer of a machine gun took up the song. It sang a few notes and then became suddenly silent. Freddy jumped out of the car and beckoned to Dave.

"We'd better take a look, Dave," he said in a worried voice. "If they are really close we wouldn't have a chance in the car. Our best bet would be to hide out in the woods until they've passed."

Dave jumped down and looked into Freddy's eyes.

"You mean?" he asked in a strained voice. "You think the Sergeant bumped into them, and they killed him?"

"I'm afraid so," Freddy nodded and swallowed. "We'd better make sure, though. Don't you think so?"

"Okay by me," Dave said, though he didn't feel so inside. "Lead on, Freddy. I'm right with you."

CHAPTER THIRTEEN

Bombs for Namur

With the English youth picking the way, the two boys crept forward through the woods toward the spot from whence had come the sharp burst of machine gun fire. Before they had traveled a hundred yards a shout in German stopped them in their tracks.

"Just a Belgian dog!" the voice called out. "He was probably deserting, so it is well that we shot him!"

Dave's heart became icy cold in his chest yet at the same time bitter resentment toward the Nazis flamed up in his brain. Then he suddenly realized that Freddy was creeping forward on all fours, so he dropped to the ground himself and followed. At the end of a few yards they came to a break in the trees that gave them a view of a large field in the distance. Three light German tanks were parked in the field. A helmeted figure, probably an officer, was standing up in the gun turret of each. Some sixty yards in front of the tanks two German soldiers were bending over a motionless figure on the ground. It was now too dark for Dave to get a good view of the crumpled figure on the ground. But he knew he didn't need a clear view. That Belgian Sergeant would never drive them to Namur, now.

"The dirty rotters, the swine!" he heard Freddy's hoarse whisper at his side. "Three light tanks against one poor Belgian sergeant. He was a decent chap, too. Blast Hitler, I say!"

"The same for the whole bunch of them!" Dave breathed angrily. "Boy, I wish I had a machine gun right now. I'd give them plenty!"

"Not against tanks, I fancy," Freddy said. "Well, that cooks it. We've got to go it alone. Look! They're starting off again. Now, if they just head...!"

The English youth let his voice trail off, but he didn't have to finish the sentence as far as Dave was concerned. He had the same thought. If the tanks turned off to the right the scouting car would not be discovered and they could continue their journey in it. But if the tanks turned to the left, toward the woods in which they crouched, it would be good-bye scouting car. The tanks would spot it for sure, and blow it to bits with their armor piercing guns if they didn't take it for their own use.

Dave's heart seemed to stop beating, and he held his breath, as the tank engines clattered up into life and the metal clad ground bugs started to move forward. Then suddenly he wanted to yell with relief. The farthest tank from them wheeled around on its treads to the right. The second tank in line followed suit, and then the third. Making a racket that echoed and reechoed back and forth across the war swept countryside, the squadron of tanks moved out of the field, rumbled down over the lip of a slope in the ground and were soon lost to view. Dave let the air out of his lungs and whistled softly.

"Boy, is that a break for us!" he grunted. "We can use that scouting car, now."

"You're jolly well right we can!" Freddy cried and leaped to his feet. "It's a Renault, too, and I've driven Renaults lots."

"Then you're elected," Dave said. "So let's go!"

In less than a minute they were back in the scouting car and Freddy was kicking the engine into life. The instant it roared up he shifted into gear and sent the car rolling around to the left in the direction the dead Belgian Sergeant had indicated.

"I hope he knew what he was talking about!" Freddy yelled above the sound of the clashing of gears. "After that crazy ride I'm not sure at all where we are. But, I'll recognize that Namur road when we come to it. One of the few decent roads in Belgium. Well, we're off!"

The English youth punctuated the last by ramming the car into high and stepping on the gas. Dave's head snapped back and he grabbed wildly for a hold and found one.

"Gosh, you and that Sergeant!" he gasped. "But, it's okay, now. Let her rip, Freddy. Say! It's plenty different riding in the front seat of one of these things, isn't it?"

It was different, too. It was much easier on the bones and tender spots of the human body. Though the car was racing across a rough uneven surface, Dave didn't get half the bouncing around sitting up front. But suddenly when a group of trees came rushing at them and Freddy yanked down on the wheel and swerved past with but a couple of feet to spare, Dave felt his hair stand up straight on his head.

"It's fun driving one of these things!" he heard Freddy shout. "A Renault's a good bus. My father has one."

"Sure, but I'm the passenger, don't forget!" Dave shouted back. "How about some lights? It's getting pretty dark."

"I guess we'd better," Freddy replied and flicked up a switch on the dashboard.

Two pale beams of light swept out in front of the car. They helped some, but they were considerably dimmed so as not to be easily spotted from the air. And they most certainly didn't put Dave much at ease. Dark objects continued to whip into view and then go slipping by as Freddy skillfully wrenched the wheel this way or that. And then suddenly they bounced out of a field onto a dirt road. They had actually turned on to the road and were tearing along it toward the west before Dave realized they were on it.

"Holy smokes, you're good, and no fooling!" he cried. "You sure know how to drive. Well, the Sergeant was right about this road anyway. Wonder how far it is to the main road? Hey, what's the idea of stopping?"

Freddy had suddenly slammed on the brakes, swung to the side of the road, and switched off the lights.

"Planes," he said. "Hear them? They might see our lights. Thought so. They're German, and low, too!"

"And coming right toward us!" Dave said as he twisted around in the seat. "Gee, you've got ears, too!"

Throbbing, pulsating thunder was rolling toward them out of the sky. The planes were not more than a couple of thousand feet up in the sky, and from the sound there were at least a couple of squadrons of them. The two boys squinted up at the now dark sky, and then suddenly they saw the armada of wings sweeping forward against the stars. They showed no lights, but it was easy to pick them out by the bluish glow of the engine exhaust plumes trailing backward.

"Gee, there's a hundred of them, at least!" Dave breathed. "They look like Heinkels to me. Wonder where they're headed? Gosh, look at them, Freddy. Aren't they something?"

Freddy didn't reply. He sat peering up at the death armada as it winged by, and Dave suddenly saw the frown on his friend's face.

"What are you frowning about?" he asked.

"I'm wondering," Freddy replied. "Unless I'm mistaken those chaps are heading for the same place we are. Namur. Yes, I'm almost sure of it!"

"So what?" Dave murmured.

"So I fancy there'll be very little of it left," Freddy said. "I'll bet you five pounds they know Belgian G.H.Q. is at Namur, and they're going over there to knock it out. Well, all we can do is keep on going, I guess."

The roar of the bombers was fading away to the south. Freddy started the car again and switched on the lights. At the end of five minutes or so they suddenly came upon a well paved broad highway.

"That poor Belgian Sergeant was right, bless him!" Freddy shouted happily and turned south on the road.

"Yes, but look!" Dave yelled and pointed ahead. "Look at that red glow way down there. Gee, it looks like the whole horizon is on fire. And, hey! Hear that? Hear those sounds. I bet that's those planes dropping bombs."

"And I bet that's Namur!" Freddy cried and speeded up the car. "Blast it, we're too late I'm afraid, Dave. Belgian H.Q. has probably cleared out long ago. We'll never find them there, if that's Namur!"

For the next few minutes neither of the boys spoke. They both sat tense in the seat staring at the ever increasing red glow that mounted higher and higher up into the horizon sky. A red glow that was mixed with streaks of yellow, and flashes of vivid orange. And all the time the *br-r-ump! br-r-ump! br-r-ump* of detonating high explosive bombs came to them above the roar of the scouting car's engine. In a weird sort of way it reminded Dave of a movie he had once seen. He couldn't remember the title but it was a movie about the world coming to an end. The scenic effects had been like what he was witnessing now. Only they hadn't been half so vivid nor so heart chilling as this. That had been a movie. This was real war. Way off there in the distance a city was probably dying. The bombs of war-making maniacs were smashing a living city into powdery ruins. It was like a horrible nightmare. And it was, because it was true!

Freddy suddenly slowing down the car made Dave tear his eyes from the terrifying spectacle in the distance. He looked at his friend in sudden alarm.

"What's the matter, Freddy?" he asked.

The English youth pointed down the highway.

"Lights coming our way," he said. "We'd better pull over and see what's what. I was going to stop, anyway. There's something strange about this, Dave."

"Yes, and I know what you mean, too!" Dave said as he suddenly realized. "The highway's been empty ever since we came onto it. We haven't passed a thing, or met anything."

"Right you are," Freddy nodded. "I've been wondering about that. But, we're meeting something, now. I say, that's not a car. The lights aren't together. They must be motorcycles."

"They are!" Dave said. "Hear their motors? Boy, are they stepping along."

"Phew!" Freddy suddenly cried out. "Supposing they're German? We'd better hop out and...."

"Too late, now!" Dave cried as the lights swerved toward their side of the road. "They've seen our lights. And, here they are, too!"

The last word had no more than left Dave's lips than two army motorcycles roared up beside the car and brakes screamed to a halt. Dave saw two shadowy figures vault from the saddles and then the white beam of a flashlight flung straight into his face blinded him. The blood running out of his face felt like cold water. He tried to shout that they were not soldiers but the words would not come. Then he almost sobbed aloud as a sharp voice spoke in French.

"Who are you? What is this? *Nom de Dieu!* Two boys in a scouting car. Well, have you lost your tongues? What is all this, I ask?"

"We are trying to reach General Boulard's headquarters," Freddy said before Dave could open his mouth. "We have important information. Will you please take that light out of my eyes? We are not armed, as you can see."

The bright light was lowered but it was several seconds before the boys could adjust their eyes to the sudden change from brilliant light to almost pitch darkness. Then they saw two Belgian corporals with dispatch rider brassards fastened about the left sleeve of their tunics. Each had his army pistol drawn and held ready for use.

"General Boulard?" one of them grunted. "Why do you wish to see him, eh? And what are you doing in this scouting car? So you stole it, yes? And I suppose you were planning to take it to your family and fill it with your family's furniture? Well...."

"Nuts!" Dave suddenly yelled at them. "We're not Belgians. He's English, and I'm American. We've escaped from Germany with valuable information. A Belgian lieutenant gave us this car, and with a sergeant to drive it. He's back there dead. We almost bumped into three German tanks, and...."

"German tanks?" one of the dispatch riders broke in excitedly. "Where?"

"Back over there a ways," Dave said and pointed in the general direction from whence they had come. "Is General Boulard's headquarters still in Namur?"

The dispatch riders didn't answer at once. They looked at each other, shrugged, and looked quite alarmed.

"If these infants saw Boche tanks," one of them murmured, "then it must be a flanking movement to cut us off from Brussels. We must continue on at once!"

"At once!" his partner agreed and turned to his motorcycle.

"I say there, wait!" Freddy shouted angrily. "Is General Boulard at Namur?"

"There is nothing at Namur, except death and the cursed Boches!" one of the dispatch riders shouted. "We go to the General's new headquarters, now. Follow us and we will show you the way. But, hurry! If you did see tanks where you say, then we are practically surrounded by the swine. There is not a moment to lose, unless you care to be shot or at best taken prisoner by the butchers!"

As though to give emphasis to their words the dispatch riders vaulted onto their saddles and opened up their motorcycle engines in a roar of sound that seemed to bounce clear up to the stars and back again. They were off like a shot and over a hundred yards ahead before Freddy could turn the small scouting car around. But once he had it turned around the young English youth didn't waste any time. He fairly flew after the two motorcycles while Dave clung fast to the side of the car and silently marveled some more at Freddy's masterful driving.

The Belgians roared a mile up the road, then swerved off to the left onto a road that led toward the northwest.

"They're heading for Brussels, I'm pretty sure!" Freddy shouted as the wind howled past the car. "That Sergeant was right when he said it looks bad. It not only looks, but *is*!"

"The Germans sure must be pretty deep into the country," Dave agreed. "They.... Hey, Freddy! Gosh ... look! The whole road is exploding! *Freddy...!*"

The road ahead had suddenly burst open to spout a sea of blinding light and crashing sound. The two dispatch riders seemed to melt into it and disappear. Invisible hands grabbed hold of the small scouting car and tossed it straight up into the air. From a million miles away Dave heard Freddy screaming his name. Then he had the feeling of spinning end over end off through space that was filled with white hot fire and billowing thick black smoke. A hundred million wild, crazy thoughts whirled around in his brain, and then everything turned black, and became as silent as the grave.

CHAPTER FOURTEEN

Orders from Headquarters

It was a kindly face, and the smile was warm and friendly, yet somehow Dave Dawson couldn't keep it in focus. It would be close to him one moment and seem very real. Then a cloud would pass across in front of it and the face would fade out completely. He felt as though he had been trying to hold that face in his vision for years and years. He knew that the mouth was talking to him, too, but he couldn't hear a word.

Everything was so still and quiet about him, and so white. Everything that his eyes could see was white ... except that kind looking face. He'd stare at it hard, trying to bold it in focus, and then his eyes would become so heavy, and his brain would become so sleepy. He guessed that was the trouble; why he couldn't keep seeing that face for very long at a time. He'd fall off to sleep.

Or was he actually asleep all the time and was this a dream? But why was he sleeping? He shouldn't be sleeping. He remembered, now! He and Freddy were following those two Belgian dispatch riders toward General Boulard's headquarters. Something funny, though, had happened. What could it have been? Surely he hadn't just fallen off to sleep while Freddy stuck to the wheel. *No*, of course not! More of it was coming back! There had been a terrific explosion in the road ahead, and the two dispatch riders had disappeared right into it. Yes, he remembered now what had happened. But, where was he? Why was everything white? Why was that kind looking, smiling face fading away from him so often? And why couldn't he hear those words the moving lips were saying? Was he dead? Was this what it was like when you died? And Freddy! Where was his pal, Freddy Farmer? He tried to find suitable answers in his brain, but his head ached so, and looking at that fading face made him so sleepy ... so sleepy....

And then after a long time the face suddenly stopped fading away into the depths of foggy mist. It stayed right where it was, and when the lips moved he actually heard what they said.

"How do you feel, my lad?" they said. "Does your head hurt very much?"

His head? Why should those lips ask if his head hurt? His head didn't hurt at all! As a matter, of fact, nothing about him hurt. He felt fine. He felt swell. What was going on, anyway? Holy smokes! He was in a bed. Under sheets and blankets, and everything. He pushed himself up on his elbow as easy as pie, and looked around. He saw that he was in a hospital. There was a long line of beds down each side of the huge room painted so white it almost hurt your eyes. And there was a man, a soldier in every bed because he could see the uniforms hanging on the hooks on the wall. And that face! It belonged to a captain in the British Army. The medical corps! The insignia was on the lapels of his tunic.

"Steady, my lad!" the officer cautioned in a soothing voice. "Tell me, how's the head feel? The pain gone, sonny?"

Dave blinked and was somehow a little startled to realize that he could talk. He vaguely remembered something about trying to talk a little while ago but being unable to utter a word.

"My head's okay, sir," he said. "I feel great. Where am I, anyway? And what's it all about? This is a hospital, isn't it?"

The medical officer let out a great sigh as though he had been holding his breath for a long time.

"Good, splendid!" he finally said. "You're out of it at last. You'll be all right, now, my lad. But you jolly well had a close one, I can tell you! Might have remained in a coma for weeks, and months. A ticklish thing, concussion shock. Want something to eat?"

"Sure, sure," Dave replied absently. "But, hey, I remember, now. Where's my pal? Where's Freddy Farmer? He was with me when that road exploded!"

"Road exploded, eh?" the medical officer said and raised an eyebrow. "A land mine, probably. So your friend's name is Freddy Farmer? An English lad, isn't he?"

"And the very best!" Dave said with feeling. "But where is he? Gosh, sir, please tell me! I've got to know. He's ... he's all right?"

The officer leaned down and patted his shoulder.

"Your little friend's quite all right," he said and pointed to Freddy Farmer asleep in the next bed. "He came out of it for the last time a few hours ago, but he started raving about a lot of crazy things, so I gave him something to make him sleep some more. He'll be fit as a fiddle when he wakes up. Now, what about this land mine ... or the road exploding, as you say?"

"I don't know exactly," Dave said. "Freddy was driving the Belgian scouting car, and we were following a couple of dispatch riders to General Boulard's headquarters. We had just turned off the Wavre-Namur road, I guess it was, when*blamm*! Everything went dark. But how'd we get here? Somebody picked us up last night? Hey, what's so funny about that?"

The officer wiped a broad smile from his lips.

"I wasn't laughing at you, my lad," he said. "It's amusing, though, to witness the final effects of concussion shock. My boy, you weren't picked up last night. You've been here in this British military hospital, at Lille, for eight days!"

Dave was speechless. His eyes widened in blank amazement. He just couldn't believe he had heard correctly. Surely his ears must be playing him tricks. *Eight days?*

"That's right, my lad," the medical officer said, reading Dave's bewildered thoughts. "It's exactly eight days this morning, since they brought you two in here."

"But eight days?" Dave cried. "But ... but I'm not even hurt! There are no bandages on me, and I don't ache any place. How could I have been here for eight days?"

"I'll not give you the medical explanation, because you wouldn't understand, probably," the officer said with a smile. "But what happened, was something like this. The concussion shock of that explosion, whatever it was, temporarily paralyzed certain nerve centers in your body and in your head. Why you didn't receive physical injury is just one of those mysterious things that happen often in war. A shell can blow every strip of clothing off a soldier's back, blow off his shoes, and toss him fifty yards, but not mark him with a single scratch. That's what must have happened to you and your friend. Perhaps, too, being in the scouting car protected you from things flying around. But, certain nerve centers were paralyzed. There's little we can do for that outside of a few injections. It's up to the patient's make-up, his constitution, and such. You probably don't remember waking up several times, do you?"

Dave shook his head.

"No sir," he said. "But I sort of half remember something about seeing a face that kept fading out, and seeing lips move, but I couldn't hear the words."

"Yes, that's the way it is usually," the medical officer said and nodded. "That was just parts of the nerve system returning to normal. You could see a little but you couldn't hear. Or you could feel but still not have the power to speak. The medical term for that has thirty-six letters, I believe. I don't even think I could pronounce it correctly now, anyway. But, you're fit now, my lad. I'll have the nurse bring you in something to eat."

"Gosh!" Dave gasped as a sudden thought struck him. "Have I gone eight days without eating?"

"Hardly," the other said with a laugh. "No, several times you both woke up enough to take food, though of course you don't remember it. The rest of the time we gave you injections. But, my word, the things you two raved about! You insisted, rather your friend insisted on seeing General Caldwell, Chief of Staff. You claimed you had been prisoners in Germany, and had seen a very important map. Your friend was very annoyed when we refused to summon the General at once, and gave him something to put him to sleep, instead. Really...!"

"But that's true, that's true!" Dave burst out. "We were prisoners, and we saw a map of the German plan of invasion. We escaped to the Belgian lines in a plane we stole. Then the sergeant driving us to Namur was killed. We met some Belgian dispatch riders and they were showing us the way to

General Boulard's headquarters when the whole road exploded. It's true, sir!"

The medical captain's eyes were now the size of saucers. He stood staring down at Dave in confounded amazement.

"I say, my lad, go a bit easy," he began. "I guess you're not yet out of that coma. Now, just lie back, and...."

"I'm fine, I'm okay!" Dave shouted excitedly. "Honest! It's all true, sir."

The officer continued to stare at him in puzzled bewilderment, and then Freddy's voice from the next bed caused them both to look his way.

"I say, hello, Dave!" the English youth cried. "They said you were all right, and then I guess I fell asleep again. Good grief, this is a hospital, isn't it? By George, it all comes back to me now! That road blowing up. But how in the world did we get here?"

The medical officer didn't bother to answer the question. He hurried over to Freddy's bedside and took a good look at him. Freddy gave him a puzzled frown, then his face suddenly lighted up.

"I say, I've seen you before, haven't I, sir?" he asked.

"This morning," the medical man nodded. "Then you're all ship shape, too? But, listen, my lad, do you two still insist upon seeing General Caldwell, Chief of British Staff?"

Asking the question was like turning a magic key in Freddy. The English youth became very excited at once, and breathlessly explained everything in more detail than had Dave.

"Yes sir," he finished up. "We have some valuable information, I'm sure. If you could loan us a car, sir, and tell us where we can find the General, we'll go at once."

"You two will go nowhere just now!" the officer said sternly. "Bless my soul, after what you've been through? Certainly not! However, there may be something to all this. I'll get the General on the wire and tell him about you two. His headquarters are not far away. He'll send one of his Staff, or perhaps come himself. This whole thing is almost fantastic! You're sure you're not trying to pull my leg, fool me?"

"Word of honor, sir," Freddy said solemnly.

The medical officer scowled and hesitated a moment. Then he shrugged and hurried out of the ward.

Dave looked at Freddy and grinned happily.

"Boy, am I glad to see you!" he exclaimed. "According to the Doc we should be dead, by rights, or something. Instead, we just got our nerve centers knocked haywire. Say, do you know how long we've been here? Did he tell you when you woke up last time?"

"I guess he didn't have the chance," the English youth said with a wry grin. "I started yelling for them to take us to the General, and they thought I was completely off my topper. Stuck a needle in me and I popped off like a kitten. We've been here last night or since this morning, haven't we? And where the dickens are we, anyway?"

"Hold your hat, Freddy, here it comes," Dave said with a chuckle. "We've been here eight days, he told me."

Freddy's jaw dropped and his eyes bugged out so far you could have knocked them off like marbles on sticks. Then he flushed and laughed scornfully.

"Come off it, Dave!" he protested. "Don't give me any of that kind of tosh. My word! Eight days, my hat!"

"No kidding, that's what he said," Dave insisted. And then he started to give Freddy the medical officer's description of what had happened to them, and their unknown, to them, actions during the eight day period.

He had almost finished when the medical captain came hurrying back into the ward. At his heels were two male orderlies in hospital white. Dave broke off what he was saying and stared questioningly. The medical officer looked very much excited, and also very much impressed.

"Take them to my receiving office," he said to the orderlies and stepped to the side.

Neither Dave nor Freddy had the chance to ask the questions that hovered on their lips. The orderlies took hold of their beds and started wheeling them down the aisle to the double doors at the end. They passed through another ward and then were wheeled into a fair sized room that was fitted up more as an office than a hospital room.

"That's fine," the captain said. "Return to your wards now."

The orderlies retreated and the captain looked at Dave and Freddy in surprise and admiration.

"Well, bless me!" he exclaimed. "I certainly didn't know I had two young heroes under my charge. I had thought you were just two lads caught up in the rush of things. General Caldwell is rushing over here, now, by car. He has heard about you two."

"About us?" Dave gasped. "But, heck, how could he have heard about us?"

"Yes!" Freddy exclaimed in a tone of awed wonder. "How could he have heard of us?"

"Through the Belgian High Command, I believe," the captain said. "It seems that Belgian infantry lieutenant reported your little flying incident to his commander. Also what you had told him. It was passed on up until it reached General Boulard. General Boulard, it seems, contacted General Caldwell to see if you lads had gotten through to him. The lieutenant, of course, did not know what had happened to you after you drove off in the scouting car with the Sergeant. But, I can tell you, General Caldwell is most anxious to meet you. By jove, he almost broke my ear drums with his shouting. Yes, I fancy that you two chaps are rather famous, now, you know?"

"Rot, sir," Freddy said with true British modesty. "I fancy any one could have done it. And a much better job of it, too. Is it true, sir, that we've been here eight days?"

"And nights, as well," the medical officer nodded. "But don't look alarmed, my lad. That sort of thing is not unusual. And you're both safely out of it, now. A day or two of rest, and all the food you can eat, and you'll be like new again."

"I'm okay, right now," Dave said stoutly. "But there's something you didn't explain, sir, How did we get here? Who found us, and what?"

"It's a bit sketchy," the medical officer said with a frown. "As far as I could learn a Belgian ambulance driver came across you and saw that you both weren't dead, and put you in his bus. His own hospital was being evacuated because of shell fire, and so he continued on westward. He reached a receiving station of ours and dumped his load there. You two, and three Belgian gunners. Anyway, from that point you were brought here to me. And here you are. It was something like that, anyway. Doubtless you'll never know the real facts. But, I certainly shouldn't worry about that, if I were you. Simply bless your lucky stars, and let it go at that."

"Jeepers!" Dave breathed softly. "Lucky stars? I must have a million of them, I guess. You, too, Freddy. Right?"

"Quite!" The English youth nodded. "Dashed if it isn't like some fairy tale one of those writer chaps would think up."

"And how!" Dave grunted and shook his head. "My gosh! A Stuka bomb drops on me and I wake up hours later and miles away. Then a land mine, or something, blows up in my face, and I wake up *eight days* later, and gosh knows *how* far away. I sure do get around."

"Well, better not make a habit of it, my lad," the medical officer chuckled. "The third time, you know?"

"Hey, those eight days!" Dave suddenly exclaimed. "What's been happening? Who's winning? Are the Allies beating up the Germans? Gee, I sure hope so!"

The smile fled from the medical officer's face and he became very grave. He opened his mouth to speak, but closed it abruptly. At that moment the office door swung open and a group of five tired eyed British officers entered the room. A big man, with coal black hair and steel grey eyes, led the party. Even without looking at his uniform with its rows of decoration ribbons, and high rank insignia, Dave knew at once that the man was General Caldwell, chief of British Staff. The captain swung around and clicked his heels.

"Ah, there you are, sir," he greeted the General. "And here, sir, are your two young lads. This is the American chap, Dave Dawson. And this is one of our own lads. Freddy Farmer. Boys, General Caldwell, chief of British Staff. You'd like me to retire, sir?"

"No, no, of course not, Captain," General Caldwell said in a brisk tone. Then turning his steel grey eyes on the boys he smiled faintly. "So, you are the two, eh?" he said. "I've heard quite a bit about you. Now, who wants to talk first? I want to hear everything."

"You tell him about it, Freddy," Dave said promptly. "You remembered more things on that map than I did, anyway."

Freddy flushed and looked embarrassed. The General smiled and perched himself on a corner of the bed, while his officers gathered around.

"All right, Freddy," he said. "Freddy Farmer, isn't it? Oh yes, of course. All right, Freddy, let's have it, eh?"

"Yes sir," the English youth said, and began talking in a low but clear voice.

Dave Dawson

CHAPTER FIFTEEN

Belgium Gives Up!

As Freddy recounted their experiences one by one Dave checked them in his own mind. Presently, though, he only half listened to his pal. He became fascinated looking at the British Chief of Staff. Many times he had seen General Caldwell's picture in the papers back home. And he had read a lot of the General's reputation as a fighter and leader of men. It thrilled him through and through to see the great man sitting just a few feet from him. It was another great experience he would remember always.

The one thing that pleased Dave most about the famous general was that he looked exactly like what Dave had always believed a general should look like. Tall, strong looking, and a face that could be stern and hard as rock. Right now the General could indeed be made entirely of solid rock. He didn't so much as blink an eye as Freddy talked. Not a muscle in his face moved. And his steel grey eyes instead of looking into Freddy's, looked at Freddy's lips as though to draw the words out. He remained that way right up until Freddy had spoken his last word. Then General Caldwell took his eyes off Freddy's lips and stared unblinkingly at the opposite wall.

"Well done, lads," he suddenly said, speaking in a soft voice that seemed strange coming from his stern looking face. "I'll certainly see that others hear of this, you can mark my words. And you, America! Dave Dawson, can you add anything to the story?"

Dave furrowed his brows in thought for a moment, then shook his head.

"No, guess not, General," he said. "Except that Freddy didn't tell you half of the things he did to get us out of jams. He...."

"Rot!" Freddy snorted. "Who got us out of that room? And who flew that plane and didn't break our necks, I'd like to know?"

"Yeah?" Dave grinned at him. "Well, who stopped the sergeant from running us smack into those Germans? And who stopped those wild Belgians from stabbing us with their bayonets? And who drove that scouting car when the sergeant had been killed? And who...?"

"All right, all right, boys!" General Caldwell broke it up. "You both did splendid jobs, and that's fine. And now, about that map. Let's go back to that. Just a minute."

The General turned and looked at one of his officers.

"Let's have that map, Saunders," he said.

A major whipped a rolled map from under his arm and passed it over. Another officer got a table and moved it between the two beds. A third officer dug up thumb tacks some place, and the General unrolled the map and tacked it flat on the table.

"Now," he said in his soft voice and leaned over the map. "This little town here. It's named Spontin. Do you remember if there was a colored pin there?"

The boys bent over and peered at the place on the map where the General had put a finger tip. Freddy answered first.

"Yes sir," he said. "There was a blue pin there. In fact, sir, there were three blue pins all in a line. About a quarter of an inch apart. I remember that distinctly."

"I see," the General murmured. "And do you recall if there was a date printed under those pins?"

"Yes, there was!" Dave cried. "Wait a minute. Yes, it was May Sixteenth. I'll bet on it!"

"No need of that, my boy," General Caldwell said quietly, and moved his finger. "Now, here. At Vervins, in France. What about that?"

"A blue pin also, sir," Freddy spoke up. "And the date marked under it was May Eighteenth."

"And here at Guise?" General Caldwell asked and moved his finger across the map again.

"Check on the blue pin!" Dave said.

"And I'm pretty sure that date was May Nineteenth, sir," Freddy said.

General Caldwell didn't move his finger any more. He straightened up and looked around at his officers. They all nodded together and looked very grave. A little bit of panic raced through Dave.

"We're all wet, General?" he blurted out. "You think we've just made all this up? So help me, honest, we...."

Dave cut himself off short as the Chief of Staff shook his head and gave him the ghost of a smile.

"On the contrary, not at all, my boy," he said. "As they would say in the States, I was just checking up. You two most certainly saw the German plan of invasion attack and execution."

"We could be a bit mistaken about the dates, sir," Freddy said in a hesitating voice. "But I'm pretty sure those we gave you were correct."

"They were," the General said, and there was a faint ironic edge to his voice. "You saw what the Germans *planned* to do. We saw them *do* it! They occupied Spontin on the Sixteenth, Vervins on the Eighteenth, and Guise on the Nineteenth. That's a matter of history, now."

"Good grief!" Freddy exclaimed with a sob in his voice. "They've gained that much, sir?"

"And much more," General Caldwell said grimly and took a little box from his tunic pocket. "Now, I have a very important job for you two. Very important! A whole lot depends on your memories, so sharpen them up well. Here is a box of pins. I want you two lads to try and put a pin in this map for every pin you saw in that Intelligence map. Colors don't matter. These here are all the same. All white, as you see. Now, study this map and shake up your memories well. And here's a couple of pencils, too. Write down all the dates you can remember. And put them under the right pins, of course."

"Gosh, there must have been a couple of hundred pins on that map, sir!" Dave said in a weak voice.

"Just stick in the pins you remember," General Caldwell said quietly. "And the dates, too. All right, let's get at it, shall we?"

It was well over an hour later when Freddy and Dave leaned back from the map well nigh mentally exhausted.

"Anything else would be just a wild guess, sir," Freddy said. "I wouldn't be sure of it at all."

"Me too," Dave said. "I'd just get all balled up. Those are all I can remember."

General Caldwell seemed not even to hear them. Once again he was like something made out of solid rock. He sat forward a little, an elbow on the edge of the table and his broad chin cupped in the palm of his hand. His eyes were fixed on the map, moving from pin to pin. The other officers, and the medical captain stood like statues, almost not daring to breathe. The silence that hung over the office was so charged that Dave was filled with the crazy desire to let out a yell, just to see what would happen. But, of course, he didn't so much as let out a peep. Like the others, he waited motionless for the General to speak.

Presently the General raised his head and smiled at them.

"Yes, I most certainly will make it a point that others be told about you two," he said. "I know His Majesty King George will certainly be interested to hear it. You have done a splendid job, boys. I'm proud of you. All England will be proud of you, too. And, as you know, Freddy, England never forgets."

"But, sir," Freddy began as his face got red with embarrassment. "But, sir, if the Germans have advanced so far what good is the information we've given you? We've given it to you too late."

"In war it's never too late," General Caldwell said quietly. "True, if I could have seen the map the day you did, why, perhaps things might now be different. But even at that you can't tell. No, lad, the information has not come to me too late. In fact, it has come to me just in time. I think, boys, that this information will save a considerable part of the British Army in France and Belgium."

The General suddenly got to his feet, and Dave gulped as he saw the fiery look that leaped into the officer's eyes.

"It depends a lot on the King of the Belgians," he said as though he were talking to himself. "If he lets us down, exposes our left flank, it will be bad. But, without this information I have now, it could well be twice as bad."

"Then there's something to that rumor, sir?" the medical officer spoke up. "The Belgians may quit?"

"It's more than rumor," General Caldwell said in a hard voice. "But I pray to God they don't. Saunders! Bring this map along, will you? And Freddy, and you, Dave, it was a job well done. I'm proud of you. Very proud. You'll hear more of this, later, mark you."

As the two boys stared wide eyed and open mouthed, General Caldwell and his Staff officers clicked their heels and saluted smartly. The boys were still in their Seventh Heaven trance when the medical officer returned after seeing the General and his officers to their cars outside.

"A red letter day for you two, what?" he beamed.

Dave gulped for air and slowly came back to earth.

"Boy oh boy!" he breathed. "What do you know! A salute from a General! Gosh! Say, Captain, could we have some food, and our clothes, now, maybe?"

"All the food you can put in your stomachs," the medical officer said. "But jolly well no clothes. You two young heroes stay in bed for a few more days, at least. Mind you, now, that's an order. I may not be a general, but I'm jolly well in charge of this hospital!"

And the medical captain meant exactly what he said. Both Dave and Freddy begged and pleaded to be allowed to get up. They had found that the hospital was terribly short handed, and they were both anxious to do what they could to help. Besides, staying in bed thinking and talking, and talking and thinking was slowly driving them crazy. Regardless of what the General had said each nursed the tiny fear that they had arrived too late with their information. They now knew how far the German hordes really had smashed through toward the coast of France and Belgium, and even to their untrained minds it held horrible and terrible significance.

But the medical captain stuck to his order, and would not let them go. On the second day after the visit by General Caldwell they were allowed to get up and wander about the hospital wards at will. It was then they discovered that every one in the hospital had learned of their brave and courageous work, and the wounded soldiers heaped praises upon them from all sides. Yet, underneath the praise and the attempts by the soldiers to be cheerful, there was a note of worry, and strain, and a sort of breathless waiting. Dave and Freddy caught the feeling at once and it served to add to the doubt and fears in their own minds that all they had done, and all they had suffered had gone for nought.

Everybody was waiting, waiting. Waiting for what, they did not know. Or if they did they kept it to themselves. News of the battles sifted gradually into the hospital wards. Some of it was true, and a lot of it was false. But all of it rasped nerves and cut deep into the tortured minds of men.

And then, on the third day, it happened!

The news flew from lip to lip, and a pall of misery and bitterness hung over the entire hospital. Belgium has quit! The Belgians have thrown down their guns and given up! The whole left side of the British Army is now exposed to the Germans racing down out of Holland! On the south the French and the British have been split by a German wedge driven straight across France to Abbeville on the Channel coast. The entire British Army, and part of the French, is surrounded on three sides. There is only one door of escape left open. That door is Dunkirk!

The instant they heard the news Dave and Freddy rushed to the office of the medical captain. They found there a very worried and very harassed man. He was just hanging up on the telephone when they burst in. He saw them, started to wave them outside, but suddenly checked the motion.

"Come in, you two," he called to them. "How do you feel?"

"Swell," Dave said.

"Very fit, sir," Freddy said.

The medical officer nodded and then stared at them a moment or two and drummed nervous fingers on the top of his desk.

"You've heard the news?" he suddenly asked.

They nodded, and waited.

"It puts us in a tight corner," the officer said. "And it puts me in a *very* tight corner. I've just received orders from G.H.Q. to evacuate this hospital at once. There are over five hundred wounded men here, and only a dozen ambulances. We're to evacuate to the Base Hospital at St. Omer. Now ... You chaps told me the truth, eh? You *do* feel fit?"

"Gee, yes!" Dave exclaimed. "We came in here to see if there wasn't something we could do to help. We feel swell, honest."

"That's right, sir," Freddy nodded. "And there *is* something we can do?"

"There is," the medical officer said. "I haven't enough ambulance drivers, and we've got to get these wounded men out of here at once. Before tonight, in fact. I'll tell you the truth, boys. At the speed the Germans are advancing, now that the Belgians have given up, they'll be here in Lille, tonight!"

"Gee!" Dave breathed softly. "Right here in this place, tonight?"

The medical officer nodded and held up a hand.

"Hear those guns?" he said gravely. "They are not more than twenty miles away, and they are German. We've got to work fast, boys. Every man we have to leave here will become a German prisoner of war. I wouldn't ask you, except that the situation is desperate. By rights, you two should go along with the wounded, instead of driving them. But it is a grave emergency, and every one who can, *must* help."

"We're ready, sir," Freddy said quietly. "What are your orders?"

A smile of deep gratitude flickered across the officer's face.

"Get into your regular clothes, first," he said with a smile. "Then report to Lieutenant Baker in the ambulance parking lot by the south wing. And, thank you, boys. We'll meet again at St. Omer."

The two boys grinned, then turned on their heels and raced back to the ward for their clothes. The wounded soldiers suspected that something was up, and a hundred questions were hurled at them. They didn't bother to answer any of them. They simply piled into their clothes and hurried outside and around to the parking lot by the south wing.

"Gee, Freddy!" Dave panted as they raced along side by side. "I was afraid I was going to stay in that hospital for the rest of the war, and not get another chance to do anything."

"A bit worried, myself," Freddy said. "I was afraid that we'd done our job, and that it was all over as far as we were concerned. But, I have a feeling, Dave, that perhaps it's really just beginning for us."

And Freddy Farmer never spoke a truer word in his life, as they were both soon to realize!

CHAPTER SIXTEEN

Fate Laughs At Last

"Right you are, lad, off you go, and good luck!"

The voice of the Lille hospital orderly came to Dave as though from a thousand miles away. It came to him like a voice awakening him from a sound sleep. He lifted his head and mechanically reached for the brake lever of the Daimler built ambulance and stared out of bloodshot eyes at a scene that had become as familiar to him as his own face when he looked into a mirror. It was the dirt road that wound away from the Lille Hospital, curved about the small pond and then disappeared from view in some woods a half mile to the east.

How many times had he driven over that road today? He didn't know, and he didn't even bother to guess. Probably a hundred. Fifty at least. His brain had stopped thinking about things hours ago. For hours his actions had all been mechanical. A mechanical routine over and over again. Help fill the ambulance at the Lille Hospital. Get in behind the wheel and start the engine, and take off the brake, and shift into first. Start down the winding road and shift into second, and then into high. A stretch of brown road always in front of him. Driving, driving, always driving forward. Skirting shell and bomb craters. Pulling in under the nearest group of trees whenever he heard the deadly drone of Stuka dive bombers. Sitting crouched at the wheel while death whistled down from the sky to explode in the ground and spray slivers of screaming steel into all directions.

Climbing in back to put a slipping bandage back in place. Lighting a cigarette for some poor wounded soldier who couldn't use his hands. Giving them all a grin to cheer them up. Saying, "We'll be there in a couple of shakes," a million times. Starting on again. Stopping again. And then finally pulling into the St. Omer Hospital court. Helping to unload, and then the wild ride alone back to Lille for another load of wounded. Fifty trips? A hundred trips? He had no idea. Maybe this was his one thousandth trip. Was he asleep or awake? He wasn't sure of that, either. His body had stopped protesting against the aches and pains long ago. He simply didn't feel anything any more; didn't think anything. He only acted. He drove ... and drove ... and drove. Nothing else mattered. Nothing else mattered but doing his share to make sure that not a single helpless wounded soldier was captured by the hordes of Nazi troops streaming across northern France and Belgium in a mad race to cut off the British from the last open Channel port, Dunkirk.

As he took off the emergency brake he became conscious of somebody climbing into the seat beside him. He turned his head to stare into Freddy Farmer's haggard, dirt streaked face.

"What's the matter, Freddy?" he mumbled. "What are you doing here?"

"Start her off, Dave," came the dull answer. "This is the last load. I'm riding with you. The Captain and his staff are using my ambulance. Man, but I'm tired!"

"Check," Dave grunted and shifted into first. "The last load, huh? And it's just getting dark. Well, anyway, we licked 'em. The Nazis won't find anything there. Lean back and try to get a nap, Freddy."

"And you perhaps fall asleep at that wheel, and tip us into a ditch?" Freddy said with a forced chuckle. "No thanks. I'll stay awake and try to keep you that way, too. By the by, though, Dave. You've made more trips than anybody. Want me to drive this one?"

"Not a chance!" Dave said and suddenly realized that he was laughing for the first time in hours. "I still remember that ride you gave me in that Belgian scouting car. Nix. I'll do the driving. You just relax, Freddy. But, boy, will I be glad when this trip is over!"

"I'll be jolly well pleased, myself, you can bet!" Freddy murmured and stretched out his legs. "I think I shall sleep for another eight days, and not care a darn what the blasted Nazis do about it."

For the next twenty minutes that was the last spoken between the two. They were both too tired even to talk. Besides, there was little to talk about save the experiences they had had on the road. Those they could save until another day. And after all there was still this trip to complete. And so they rode along in silence. The sun slid down over the western lip of the world, and night and the Germans came sweeping up from the east. Dave kept his head lights switched off until it was too dangerous to continue further without them. Perhaps it had just been chance, or perhaps Goering's pilots had found out that the Lille Hospital cases were being evacuated over that road. Anyway, the Stukas and the light Heinkels had given it a terrific pounding all day long, and it was now well spotted with craters. To try to drive along it in the dark would be exactly the same as driving the ambulance over the edge of a cliff. It would be suicide, to say the least.

Dave hesitated a moment, though, with his hand on the switch and listened intently. Behind him there was the incessant dull rumble of the guns, punctuated every now and then by the loud thunder of a land mine going off. In the sky there was the drone of wings, but the droning was not close.

"Keep an eye peeled, will you, Freddy?" Dave said and turned the switch. "I've got to have lights or we'll go right into a shell hole. If you hear something coming, yell, and I'll switch off these things."

"Right-o!" Freddy called wearily and stuck his head out the door window and looked up. "All clear, now, though. None of the blighters near us. I say, what's up, now?"

Dave didn't bother to answer. He, too, had spotted the waving flashlight just up the road. He slipped the car out of gear, steered it around the rim of a yawning bomb crater and let it roll to a stop. A British infantry officer, with a Military Police band on his tunic sleeve, ran up to Dave's side of the ambulance and flashed his light in Dave's eyes for a second.

"Where are you headed, lad?" he asked.

"St. Omer," Dave said. "We've got the last load of wounded from the Lille hospital."

"Well, you can't take them to St. Omer," the officer said. "A mile up ahead there's a road to the right. Take it and keep going until you're stopped. Whoever stops you will give you further directions. All right, off with you. Good luck."

"But, hey, why not St. Omer?" Dave blurted out. "We've been taking them there all day."

"I know," the officer said in a half angry and half bored voice. "But they've all been evacuated again. To Dunkirk. Hitler's lads are in St. Omer, now. Better hop it. They may be here, soon."

Dave slammed the ambulance into gear and started off. Raging anger surged up within him. He gripped the bucking wheel until his hands hurt. Nazis are here! Nazis are there! Nazis are every place! Even thinking of the name made him want to start screaming and shouting at the top of his voice. He turned his head slightly and took a quick side glance at Freddy. The English youth's chin was firm, and there was the same defiant look in his eyes. However, the droop of his shoulders spoke plainly of the bitter thoughts that were sweeping through his mind. Impulsively Dave let go a hand from the wheel for a second and slapped Freddy on the knee.

"Don't let it get you down, Freddy," he said. "They'll trim the stuffing out of Hitler before it's over."

"Of course," Freddy said in a heavy voice. "I wasn't thinking of that. If we could only have reached General Caldwell sooner."

"Gosh, we did our best!" Dave exploded. "And, besides, the General told us it helped plenty. Gee, I hope he just wasn't kidding us. I don't think so, though. A man like General Caldwell doesn't kid, I bet. Well, here's the road. Wonder where it'll take us."

They had reached the turn off. So had some Stukas a couple of hours before and they had marked it well with a cluster of bomb craters. Dave had to detour through a field to make the turn but he managed to get back onto the road. To his vast relief he found it hardly touched by bombs and he was able to speed up the ambulance. The good road helped his spirits, too. It boosted them up considerably and a lot of his fatigue fell away from him. The same was true with Freddy. The English youth continued to stare fixedly through the windshield at the glow of the headlights on the road, but his body seemed to straighten up, and there was a less depressed air about him.

However, it was as though it all had been planned by the fates controlling the war and the immediate destinies of these two brave gallant youths. It was as though it was planned for them to be lifted up in spirit, and in strength, so that they might have something left with which to face the next misfortune of the conflict to befall them.

The first indication that there was more trouble ahead came as they roared around a bend in the road, and then the road straightened out like an arrow.

"My gosh, look!" Dave cried and pointed. "Like an earthquake had hit it or something!"

Both sides of the road, as far as they could see in the glow of the headlights, were strewn with heaped up piles of war equipment wreckage. Guns from machine gun size to heavy howitzers lay scattered about. Ammunition wagons were over on their sides, their contents spilled on the ground like sand from a box. Shell blasted tanks rested in soft ground at crazy angles, some of them blown wide open, and all of them of no more use to anybody.

"Gosh, like driving through a junk yard!" Dave grunted and unconsciously slowed down the ambulance. "What do you suppose happened? Gee, that's English stuff, too. See the markings?"

"Yes," Freddy replied. "And I think I can guess what happened. A retreating British column was caught here by the bombers, I think. You can see where the craters were filled in so the rest of them could carry on. What equipment they couldn't take, they destroyed so that the Germans wouldn't get it. Look, Dave! There's another flashlight chap up ahead. And he's English! I can see him clearly, now."

"Right," Dave nodded as he too caught sight of the khaki clad figure, with an M.P. band on his arm, standing in the middle of the road.

He slipped the ambulance out of gear and let it roll to a stop and stuck his head out the door window.

"We've got wounded here!" he said as the officer moved forward. "They turned us off onto this road, back a few miles. Said the next officer we met would give us instructions."

"More wounded?" the officer echoed in an exasperated voice. "I seriously doubt if there'll be room. But get along. First turn left, and two miles straight. A railroad junction there, and still working, I certainly hope! They'll take your men. Now, chase along with you!"

"What happened here?" Dave asked and reached for the gear shift lever.

"The worst!" the officer snapped, and gestured with his hand. "Stukas caught a whole battalion. Nasty business! Now, chase, do you hear?"

Dave didn't wait to argue about that. He sent the car rolling forward and kept his eyes open for the turn to the left. He came to it presently and turned off. It was also more or less untouched by bombs so he could keep his speed steady. In almost no time they came upon a whole army of British soldiers. They jammed the road and overflowed on both sides. Hundreds of pairs of eyes were turned their way as their headlights cut through the night. A soldier with sergeant's chevrons on his sleeves rushed up to them.

"Shut off those blasted lights, you fool!" he roared. "You want the Jerry planes to ... Good grief, a couple of *kids!* What's this?"

"Ambulance with wounded from Lille, Sergeant," Freddy called out to him. "The officer back there told us to take them to the rail junction. How far is it?"

"Wounded, eh?" the sergeant grunted. "Well, that's a sight different. Keep going. You're practically there, mates."

The sergeant stepped back and cupped big hands to his mouth.

"Make way!" he thundered at the road choked mass of British troops. "Ambulance! Make way there, you chaps! Ambulance! Give them the horn, lad. That'll make 'em jump."

The sergeant barked the last at Dave as the ambulance started forward. Dave got the car in high then held his hand on the horn. Freddy got out on the running board and started shouting, "Make way for an ambulance!" at the top of his voice. For two or three awful seconds Dave was afraid that the soldiers were going to refuse to move. But the shouted word, "Ambulance!" finally did the trick. They shuffled off to both sides and left a path down the middle of the road. Driving with one hand and keeping his other on the horn, Dave steered the ambulance down that path until a bomb shattered railroad bridge stopped him. There was no need of going farther anyway.

They had reached the rail junction, or at least what was left of it. Eastward from the bridge the track was just so much twisted steel, but westward from the bridge it had not been touched, by some strange miracle. There was a long train of some twenty cars on the track with an engine at the far end. Dimmed lights were moving around all over the place like fire-flies on a muggy night. The murmur of many voices filled the air, and as Dave got his eyes accustomed to the scene he saw that long lines of battle weary soldiers were climbing into the cars. And then out of nowhere a squad of soldiers with white bands on their tunic sleeves swooped down on the ambulance.

"Shut off your motor, mate!" a voice shouted. "You won't be needing it any more. Step lively, you lads. Easy with the poor blighters, now. That's the way."

Before Dave and Freddy could climb stiff legged down from the ambulance the white banded group of soldiers had the rear doors open and were gently but swiftly lifting out the wounded on stretchers and carrying them to the train. Nobody talked. Even the wounded made no sound. Everybody seemed to realize that all that counted was speed, and they were concentrating on that alone. Dave watched for a minute or so and then went up to the soldier who had given the orders.

"Where's the train going?" he asked.

"Dunkirk, unless the Jerry fliers stop us," the soldier replied without looking at him. "Any more of these chaps coming along in back of you?"

"This is the last load from Lille," Dave said. "I don't know about any others."

"Lille?" the soldier gasped and seemed startled. "I thought the Jerries were there!"

"I fancy they are, now," Freddy spoke up. "I say, will there be room enough for us on that train, do you think?"

"Always room for two more on anything," the soldier grunted and watched the stretchers disappear into the maze of moving lights. "You chaps just follow me, and I'll...."

The soldier never finished the rest of that sentence. At any rate, if he did, the boys didn't hear him. At that moment there came the faint drone of engines high in the sky and to the east. Instantly it seemed as though a thousand men put whistles to their lips and all blew them at the same time.

"Bombers!" roared one fog horn voice.

"Everybody aboard!" bellowed another.

"Never mind your kit, you men, get aboard!" thundered a third.

"All lights out!" a fourth voice carried above all the others.

In the wink of an eye the moving lights stopped moving and went out. All was plunged into darkness. A darkness filled with grunting sounds on the ground, and the throbbing beat of approaching airplanes overhead. Instinctively Dave and Freddy grabbed hands and started moving toward the train. No sooner had they taken a dozen steps than they ran smack into a wall of solid flesh. They tried to force their way through but it was as futile as trying to push a tidal wave to one side. They alone were not the only ones trying to get aboard that train. A few hundred others had the same idea.

Suddenly the shrill whistle of the engine cut through all other sound. A moment later the angry roar from hundreds of throats told Dave and Freddy that the train was moving. They stopped trying to push forward, and simply stood there listening to the angry shouting of the troops who could not get aboard, and the sound of the train as it picked up speed and went racing off toward the east.

"Here they are! Everybody scatter!"

Perhaps it was the same fog horn voice, and perhaps it wasn't. Anyway, everybody heard the command and started moving. A moment later the air became filled with the howl of diving wings. Further orders were not necessary. In a flash Dave thought of the bomb blasted bridge. The road had once dipped down under it, but now it was no more than a cave made out of jagged chunks of stone with twisted steel rails and splintered ties for roof shingling. He grabbed Freddy by the arm and spun them both around.

"That busted bridge!" he shouted in his friend's ear. "We can crawl down under it. We should be safe."

"Just thinking of that, myself!" Freddy shouted back as they both broke into a run. "Those blasted Stukas! Will we never hear the last of them!"

As though to punctuate that sentence the leading bomber swooped low, dumped its load and went screaming up into the night sky. Its bomb struck a hundred yards away but the concussion seemed to lift both of the boys off their feet. It put wings on their feet as well. They dashed madly through the roaring darkness, missed turned-over trucks and hunks of the bombed station by inches, and finally scrambled down under the bridge and into the cave-like hole blown out of one of the supporting walls. They crawled back over the broken stones as far as they could and sat huddled together listening to the world blow apart over their heads.

"Well, at least we got our load of wounded aboard!" Dave shouted as there came a lull in the bedlam of thunderous sound. "That's something, I guess."

"Yes, we didn't let them down," Freddy's voice came faintly. "Phew, but I'm tired. Stukas or no Stukas, I don't think I can keep awake another minute."

The words seemed to touch something inside Dave. He too became suddenly listless in both mind and body. He felt Freddy sagged against him and he battled to keep his eyes open; to keep a look-out in case they might have to change their place of shelter. But ton weights hung on his eye lids, and it was impossible to keep them open any longer. Above them worlds exploded sound and flame. Underneath them worlds shook and trembled as each devastating blow was struck. None of it, however, reached the two boys. Young strong bodies had taken an awful beating for hours on end, and they needed rest. Time might cease, and the world could come to an end, but it would have no effect on Dave Dawson and Freddy Farmer, for they were both sound asleep.

CHAPTER SEVENTEEN

Thunder In The West

The cold, clammy air of early dawn finally pried Dave's eye lids open and brought him back to the conscious world. For a moment he stared dully at the mass of grey shadows all around him. Then gradually he realized that the shadows, most of them, were rocks and huge chunks of cement, and that light was filtering down through cracks and holes between them. That realization brought back memory of where he was. Then swiftly followed recollection of all that had happened and why he was there. He started to get to his feet, and his movements awakened Freddy Farmer slumped against him. The English youth groaned, opened his eyes and stared blankly around for a moment. Then they cleared as fragments of memory came racing back to him, too. He sat up and gingerly flexed his arms and legs.

"Gee, it's morning!" he exclaimed.

"And the Stukas have gone, thank goodness," Dave said. "Lets get out of here. Maybe the train's back and we can get aboard it this time. Gosh! I'm stiff as a board."

"I can hardly move!" Freddy moaned and got slowly to his feet. "Man, I never thought a chap could fall asleep while bombs were falling. My father told me that he once slept through a ten hour bombardment in front of Amiens, in Nineteen Seventeen. I aways thought he was pulling my leg, but now blessed if I don't believe him. I say, what's that?"

Dave cocked his head and listened to the sudden strange sound.

"Troops marching!" he breathed. "That's what it is. Troops marching. The train must be back. Come on, Freddy!"

Dave scrambled forward and started crawling up out of the cave and between the rocks to firm ground. He suddenly stopped short as he glanced through a crack that gave him a clear view of the road that ran along in back of the bomb shattered station. His heart leaped up into his throat, and for a second or two he couldn't utter a word. Freddy, scrambling up behind, bumped into him and started an exclamation. Dave whirled and put a silencing hand to his lips.

"Pipe down!" he hissed. "Freddy! For gosh sakes, take a look through that crack. Gee! What do you know about that?"

The English youth squirmed past him and peered out through the crack. His young body stiffened, and there was the sharp sound of sucking air into his lungs. He turned around and stared wide eyed at Dave and licked his lower lip.

"Germans!" he whispered. "The beggars are all over the place. We've been left behind, Dave. Our boys must have moved on when the Stukas went away. But we were asleep."

"Yeah, I guess that was it," Dave said and nodded. "Holy smokes, Freddy, what shall we do?"

"I don't know, except to stay where we are," the English youth replied in a tight voice. "If we show our heads they're sure to grab us. There must be thousands of them!"

"Millions, it looks like!" Dave said with a gulp. "Yes, the best thing to do is stay right here and hope they don't find us. Maybe they'll move off after awhile, then we can beat it. Gosh! I had all I want of a being a German prisoner. Sure, let's stay right here."

"At least we won't starve, no matter how long they take marching through," Freddy said. "We both have plenty of chocolate bars we got at the hospital. And I didn't have to give any of the water in my canteen to the wounded I carried. Did you?"

"Not a drop, it's full," Dave said, and patted the canteen at the end of the strap hooked over his shoulder. "You're right, we won't go hungry or thirsty. But gosh, I hope they don't stick around too long, or we'll never get out of this place. Maybe we were crazy to duck in here, huh?"

"And maybe we would have been crazier to have gone some place else," Freddy murmured and pulled a bar of chocolate from his pocket. "At least no bombs hit us here."

"That's right," Dave agreed. Then with a stiff grin, "And it's a cinch that none are going to hit us, either, while those Germans are out there. But I sure hope all those British troops got away. I guess they did, though, or we'd hear fighting right now. Gee! Can you beat it?"

"Beat what?" Freddy asked through a mouthful of crunched chocolate bar. "What's the matter?"

"I was just thinking, and maybe it isn't so funny," Dave said. "We sort of started all this business behind the German lines, and here we are again. I sure hope we don't end it that way! Wonder how long we'll have to wait? Until it's dark, I guess."

Freddy didn't answer. He crawled up the stones and peered through the crack again. When he came down his dust and dirt smeared face looked most unhappy.

"Until it's dark, at least," he said with a sad shake of his head. "And more war music, too. I just saw them wheeling some guns into position in back of the railroad station. Yes, I'm afraid the blasted beggars are planning to stay here a bit, too."

"Well, when it gets dark we get out of here," Dave said grimly. "Guns or no guns."

"You bet," Freddy said and fell silent.

As though their silence was a signal to the gunners above, the earth and the sky once more began to shake and tremble as the gun muzzles belched out their sheets of flame and steel-clad missiles of death and destruction that went screaming far off to the east. To get away from the shuddering, hammering pounding as much as possible, the two boys crawled far back into the wall cave and tried to make themselves comfortable.

Seconds clicked by to add up to minutes, and minutes ticked by to add up to an hour. Then eventually it was two hours, then three, then four. And still the guns hammered and snarled and pounded away at their distant objectives. It seemed as though it would never end. Try as they did to steel themselves against the perpetual thunder, and the constant shaking and heaving of the earth under them, it was right there with them every second of the time. Their eardrums ached, and seemed ready to snap apart. They tore off little pieces of their shirts and used them as plugs to stuff in their ears. That helped some, but it made speech between them impossible.

Roaring, barking thunder all morning, and all afternoon. But along toward evening it died down considerably. And when the shadows of night started creeping up it ceased altogether. The two boys crawled forward and up the bomb-made rock steps and peered through the crack between the stones. The hopes that had been born in them when the guns stopped seemed to explode in their brains. The guns were not being hooked onto the tractors. Nor were the swarms of troops climbing into the long lines of motorized Panzer trucks. On the contrary, mess wagons were being rolled forward, and flare lights were being set about all over the place. Even as Dave and Freddy crouched there watching with sinking spirits two flare lights sputtered into being directly above their heads. With sudden terror gripping their hearts they scuttled back deep into their hiding place.

"No soap, I guess," Dave said bitterly. "We'd stick out like a couple of sore thumbs. What do you think, Freddy?"

"The same as you," the English youth said unhappily. "We'd be fools to budge an inch. I most certainly wish we had blankets. These are the hardest rocks I ever felt."

"You said it," Dave muttered and ran his hand over the hard surface that was unquestionably going to serve as his bed for another night of terror. "Maybe, though, they'll pull out before dawn. Or maybe in the morning, for sure."

If the gods of war heard Dave Dawson's words they must have laughed loud and with fiendish glee, for they knew how false his hopes were. The Germans did not leave during the night. Nor did they leave in the morning.

As soon as it was dawn they started their devastating bombardment again. And for another whole day the boys huddled together in their hiding place and struggled with every bit of their will power to stop from going stark, raving mad from the thunder of the guns.

Then, suddenly, when there was still an hour of daylight left, the guns went silent for keeps, and instead there were all kinds of sounds of feverish activity. Harsh orders flew thick and fast. Men shouted and cursed. Tractor engines roared into life. Truck transport gears were meshed in nerve rasping grinding sound, and as the boys watched through their look-out crack they saw the Germans move slowly off down a road leading toward the southwest. Neither of them spoke until the last truck had passed out of view. And by then it was pitch dark, save for a shimmering red glow to the east and to the south.

"Boy, I thought it would never happen!" Dave said in a shaky voice. "Come on! Let's get going before others arrive here. Which way do you think we'd better head?"

"The railroad track, I think," Freddy said after a moment of silence. "It must have been blown all to bits by those Stukas, or else there would have been a train come up to take those Germans away. Instead, though, they headed down the road to the southwest."

"Check," Dave said. "And that track is supposed to lead to Dunkirk. Gosh, I hope the British are still there."

"They must be there," Freddy said firmly. "You can still hear the guns up ahead, so there must be somebody besides Germans around. I say, look at that fog, or is it fog? Yes, it is. And it's beginning to rain, too. Well, thank goodness for that. We won't be seen or heard so easily. Right-o, Dave. Let's get on with it. Like the chaps in the R.A.F. say, Tally-ho!"

"Tally-ho!" Dave echoed happily and started scrambling up out of the cave.

Walking side by side, and gripping hands to hold up the other fellow in case he slipped and started tumbling into a bomb crater, the two boys struck out boldly along the single line of track. Before they had traveled a hundred yards the railroad tracks stopped being what they were supposed to be. They became a long stretch of twisted steel and pulverized ties. But though the road bed was constantly pock marked with bomb craters it served as a guide eastward for their crunching footsteps.

Layers of fog came rolling in from the east, and with every step a fine chilling rain sprayed down upon them. But rather than being annoyed and uncomfortable, they were buoyed up by the miserable weather. It gave them added protection from any German patrols in the neighborhood. It hid them from the rest of the world of dull constant sound, and the shimmering glow of red to the east and to the south. There was more sound, and a more brilliant glow of red to the south, and as they heard it and saw it their hearts became even lighter. If there was all that sound to the south it must mean that the Germans had not been able to cut off the retreating armies at Dunkirk. And of course that was true, for as they trudged and stumbled along the bomb blasted strip of spur railroad track some fifty thousand do or die British soldiers were holding back the savagely attacking German hordes at Douai, and at the Canal de Bergues, so that some three hundred and thirty thousand of their comrades might escape the trap from Dunkirk and reach England in safety.

Of course Dave and Freddy didn't know *that* at the time. Yet, perhaps they sensed it unconsciously, for their step did become faster, their hearts lighter, and the hope they would get through somehow mounted higher and higher in their thoughts. And so on and on they went. A thousand times they stumbled over things in the darkness; went pitching together down into bomb craters, or barked their shins and raised lumps on their tough bodies. Always forward, though. They stopped talking to conserve their energy, for they had no idea how many miles of bomb blasted roadbed lay ahead of them. The fog and the rain dulled the sound of the guns so that they couldn't tell if they were drawing nearer or actually heading away from them. And although they looked at it a million times apiece the dull red glow ahead of them seemed always to remain the same. It never once brightened up or faded down. It got so that it seemed as though they were walking on a treadmill. Walking, walking, yet never seeming to get any place. Never seeing anything different to give them proof they had covered ground. Every piece of twisted track they stumbled over was the same as the last. A bomb crater into which they fell sprawling was no different from all the others. And the darkness, the fog, the rain, the boom of the guns, and the shimmering red glow were always the same in the next second, in the next minute, and in the next hour.

Grit, courage, and a fighting spirit resolved never to give up, forced them forward foot after foot, yard after yard, and mile after mile. Even thoughts ceased to stir in their brains, and there was nothing there but the fierce burning flame that drove their tired legs and bodies forward.

Then, suddenly, their separate worlds seemed to shatter before their eyes in an explosion of sound. To Dave it seemed close to an eternity before the sound made sense in his dulled brain. Then in a flash he realized that nothing had exploded. A loud voice not three feet in front of them had bellowed out the challenge.

"*Halt!*"

Even then neither of the boys could grasp its true meaning. The voice shattered their hopes, gripped their hearts with fingers of ice, and seemed to drain every drop of blood from their bodies. Fate was having the big laugh on them at last. The worst, the one thing they had dreaded had come to pass. They had stumbled headlong into a nest of Germans!

"Halt, you blighters, 'fore I run this through your bellies!"

Then truth crashed home, and the boys let out a gurgling cry of relief as they realized the voice was *speaking in English!*

CHAPTER EIGHTEEN

Wings of Doom

"Hold it!" Dave heard his own voice cry out in the darkness. "We're not Germans!"

"No!" Freddy choked out. "We're English and American! Are we near Dunkirk?"

There was a startled exclamation in the rain and fog, then the tiny beam of a buglight caught them in its glow. The light shook and there was a gasp of dumbfounded amazement.

"Strike me pink!" exclaimed the voice in back of the light. "What are you two young nippers doing here? And where'd you come from?"

The buglight was lowered and the two boys saw the dim outline of a British Tommie. His gas mask and ration kit were slung over his shoulder, and in his hands he carried a rifle with a wicked looking bayonet.

"We're trying to reach Dunkirk," Freddy spoke up. "We've been hiding for the last two days at a railway junction called, Niort, I think it was. Part of the sign had been blown away but I think that's what it was."

"Niort?" the British soldier gasped. "Come off it, now, me lad! If you were at Niort how'd you get here? I suppose by a blinking train, eh?"

"No, we walked," Dave said. "Along what was left of the railroad. We missed the last train two nights ago. It pulled out when some Stukas arrived."

The British soldier whistled through his teeth, and flashed his buglight on them just to make sure he wasn't talking to a couple of ghosts.

"Well, can you beat that!" he ejaculated. "So you were left behind with the others, eh? I was on that blinking train, thank my lucky stars! The lads that were left had to march it all the way, and with Jerry throwing everything he had at them, too. Strike me pink! You know what you two nippers have done?"

"Sure," Dave said. "Walked about a million miles, the way we feel."

"It's closer to eighteen or nineteen, lad," the Tommie said. "But that ain't the half of it. You've walked *right through* the blessed German line, that's what you've done! Right through their blinking lines, and them not knowing about it! By George, will I have a tale to tell the lads at the pub if I ever get back home!"

"But how far are we from Dunkirk?" Freddy asked. "And is there any way to get there besides walking? I don't think I can go another step."

The soldier jerked a thumb over his shoulder.

"See them flames?" he said. "That's Dunkirk. About two miles it is. And it's time for me to go in from my patrol anyway. I got a motor-bike and sidecar over there, yonder. You two can ride in the car. But we'd better hop it. It's getting toward dawn and the Stukas will be coming over to raise merry Ned. But, wait a minute, mates. Who are you and what were you doing at Niort? Why, you ain't even in uniform."

"This is Dave Dawson, an American," Freddy said. "And my name is Freddy Farmer. We've been trying to get back to England for days, and...."

"*What's that?*" the soldier cut in excitedly. "Dawson and Farmer? The couple of American and English nippers, that stole a plane and all the rest of it? Blimey! Why didn't you say so? Why you lads are heroes! The whole blinking army's been talking of what you nippers did. Come along! If there's two lads that's going to get a boat ride back home, it's you. Yes, by George! I'm that anxious to get back home so's to tell the lads, I'm fair ready to swim the blinking Channel, orders or no orders. Come along!"

Without waiting for either of the boys to so much as open their mouths the soldier grabbed them each by the arm and hurried them off through the dark to the right. He must have known the way well, for they didn't bump into a single thing. Presently he let go of them and dived into some bushes. He was out in almost no time pushing an army motorcycle and sidecar. He slung his rifle over his shoulder and straddled the seat.

"Hop in, lads!" he barked as he kicked his engine into life. "And hang on for your lives. The beach where they're taking them off onto the ships ... and man, they're bringing over anything that can float ... is on the far side of town. But the blinking town's afire, and we have to go right through it. Here we go, and a double-double to the blasted Jerries!"

Though the two boys had wedged themselves down tight in the sidecar, the soldier tore off in such a rush that he practically rode right out from under them. Yelling any complaints would have been just a waste of breath. Besides, the soldier wouldn't have heard them in the roar of his engine. So the boys simply concentrated on trying to stay in the sidecar, and breathed a prayerful hope that the soldier was an expert driver.

He was more than that. He was a miracle man on a motorcycle. He raced through the darkness without slackening his speed the fraction of a mile. The rain slithered down and the street glistened in the faint glow of his dimmed light. It looked like so much slippery black ice, and a hundred times Dave closed his eyes and waited for the sickening crash that never came. When, he dared open them again they were still hurtling forward making as much noise as a whole division of tanks.

The two miles to the ancient Channel city of Dunkirk was covered in just about as many minutes. In the last hundred yards the fog seemed to come to an end, and the rain to pass on behind them. Dave looked ahead and caught his breath sharply. Dunkirk looked like one gigantic horizon-to-horizon wall of licking tongues of flame and billowing smoke that towered high up into the sky. It was as though he had walked out of a dark room straight into the open mouth of a blast furnace. He impulsively cast a quick side glance at the soldier astride the motorcycle seat expecting to see an expression of alarm and dismay pass across the lean unshaven face. But no such thing did he see. The soldier simply lowered his head a bit, and the corners of his eyes tightened.

"Hang on, lads!" he bellowed without taking his eyes off the road. "Here comes the first of it, and it ain't no ice box!"

No sooner had the last left his lips than the heat of the flaming buildings seemed to charge forward right into their faces. Dave and Freddy ducked their heads as the soldier had done, and in the matter of split seconds they had the sensation of hurtling straight across the mouth of a boiling volcano that shot up tongues of flame on all sides.

"Lean to the right, we're turning that way!" came the soldier's yell.

They leaned together and the motorcycle and sidecar went careening around the corner of a street. It seemed to hesitate halfway around and start to slide. But the driver skillfully checked the slide with a vicious motion on the wheel, and they went roaring up a smoke filled street. A moment or two later the driver yelled for them to lean again. They did. In fact they did it no less than a dozen times during the next few minutes. And all the while the heat of the flames beat in at them from all sides, and the crash of falling walls, or of delayed action bombs going off, was constant heart freezing thunder in their ears.

Then suddenly they shot right through the middle of one final wall of fire and burst out onto a stretch of hard packed sand. It was several seconds before the heat left them and they felt rain soaked salt air strike against their faces. They gulped it into their lungs, and then both cried out in alarm as a squad of British soldiers seemed to rise right out of the sand in front of them. Their driver instantly stood up on his foot plates and roared above the sound of his engine.

"Out of the way!" he bellowed. "A couple of young heroes to get boat tickets from his nibs, the Commandant!"

Perhaps the group of soldiers heard him, or perhaps they just naturally didn't want to run the risk of being bowled over by the on-rushing motorcycle. Anyway they leaped to the side and the driver and the two boys went banging on by without a single check in the speed. After another moment or so the soldier cut his engine, slammed on his brake and slid around to a full stop as his tires sent a shower of wet sand into the air.

"There you are, nippers!" he cried and vaulted from the seat. "How was that for a bit of a joy-ride, eh? She's a good little motor bike, she is. A bit slow, but she'll do. Now, wait half a minute while I go see if the Commandant's about. Sit tight. I'll be right back."

He flung the last back over his shoulder as he went racing off to the left. Neither Dave nor Freddy said anything. They were too busy fighting to get their breath back, and to unwedge themselves from the sidecar. Eventually they were out on the sand and feeling themselves all over just to make sure no arms or legs or anything had been left behind.

"Jeepers, jeepers!" Dave finally broke the silence. "You and that Belgian sergeant are just beginners compared to that guy. My gosh! I know darn well he must have gone right through some of those buildings, instead of around them. Gee, Freddy! Look at those flames! No wonder you could see them for miles. The whole town's going up in smoke."

"Yes, but look there, Dave!" Freddy cried and grabbed his arm as he pointed with his other hand. "There on the beach. It's the British army. Look! They're even wading out in the water to the boats! It must be too shallow for them to get in any closer. Gee, Dave, *gee!*"

Dave couldn't speak as he stared at the sight. The words were all too choked up inside of him to come out. The whole beach was practically covered with row after row of British and French soldiers. They stood in long columns of ten and twelve men across, and those columns stretched from high up on the beach far out into the shallow water. In some places cars, and tanks, and trucks, anything on wheels had been driven out into the water and parked side by side, parked hub to hub and planks laid across the tops of them to form a makeshift pier that could reach out into deeper water. But there were only a few of such piers. Most of the columns of men were wading out into the water until it came up to their chests, and even up to their necks.

And out there looking weird and grotesque in the glow of the burning Channel port were boats of every conceivable description. There were row boats, and yachts. Fishing smacks and pleasure yawls. Coastal vessels and ferry boats. Motor boats and canoes. Barges and British destroyers. Anything and everything that could float had been brought over to help in the evacuation. No, it wasn't the British Navy taking the British Army home. It was all England come to rescue her fighting men.

Dave and Freddy stood rooted in their tracks staring wide eyed at the historic event that will live forever in the minds of men. Their eyes soaked up the scene, and their ears soaked up the conglomeration of sound. Oddly enough, practically all of the sounds came from off shore. The blast of whistles, the blowing of signal horns, the purr and the roar of engines, and the shouts of the appointed and of the self-made skippers and crews of the fantastic rescue fleet. The troops hardly made any sound at all. Perhaps they were too tired. Perhaps the roar of battle still ringing in their ears momentarily stilled their tongues. Or perhaps they were content just to follow the next man ahead and pray silently that they would be taken aboard some kind of a boat and sailed away before daylight and the Stukas arrived once again. But the real reason for their strange silence, probably, was because most of them had been there for days waiting their turn, and dodging Stuka bombs and bursting shells. And after such an ordeal they were too stunned to know or even care about talking. Each had a single, all important goal. A boat of some kind. And they slogged and sloshed toward it, numb to all that was going on about them.

"It's ... it's almost as though it isn't real!" Dave heard himself whisper aloud. "It's like being at a movie, and seeing something you know was just made up. Gosh, there's thousands of them. Thousands! I wonder how many have got away already? And...."

The last froze on Dave's lips. At that moment above the crackling and sullen roar of the flames devouring the city there came the dreaded sound. It was like the drumming moan of night wind in the trees, only it wasn't. It was a sound that chilled the blood of every man on shore and off shore. It was Goering's Stukas and Heinkels and Messerschmitts coming up with the rising dawn. For a long second Dave and Freddy heard it, and then it was drowned out by the mounting groans and curses that welled up from the throats of those thousands of soldiers on the beach. Yet as Dave stared at them, unable to move, he saw that not a man broke ranks. Everybody stayed in his place, as though they were on a parade ground instead of on a beach strewn with their own dead. Rifles and portable machine guns were grabbed up and pointed toward the fast lightening heavens, but no man gave up his place in line.

And then the winged vultures under Goering's command came howling down out of the sky. Their noise drowned out all other noises, including the noise of the guns that greeted them. It was as though some mighty giant were tearing the roof right off the top of the world. It wasn't a scream, and it wasn't an earth trembling wail. Nor was it a continual thunderous roar. It was just a sound that had never been heard before, and, perhaps, will never be heard again. A mighty collection of all sounds in the whole world blended into one mighty inferno of noise.

As Dave and Freddy stood transfixed it didn't so much as even occur to either of them to run for some kind of shelter. Their feet were lumps of lead and the ground was one great magnet that held them fast. Something spewed up orange and red flame a couple of hundred yards away from them. It was a bomb exploding, but they couldn't even hear the sound. Another fountain of flame, and sand showering down over everything, but no individual sound of the bomb going off. A part of the sky overhead turned into a great raging ball of red fire. It tore their eyes upward in time to see a Heinkel bomber outlined in livid flame. Then it was engulfed by that flame and came hurtling down to hit the water off-shore and disappear as though by magic.

It was then, and then only they realized that not all of the planes overhead were German. It was then they saw British Hurricanes, and Spitfires, and Defiants slash down out of the dawn sky in groups of three and pounce upon the German planes in a relentless, furious attack that set them to shouting wildly at the top of their voices. The Royal Air Force. The R.A.F., the saviors of Dunkirk! Outnumbered by the German planes, but so far above them in fighting heart, in spirit, and in real flying ability that there wasn't even any room left for comparison. A British plane against five Germans, against ten, or against fifty! What did it matter? There were gallant troops to be evacuated back home. There were fleet after fleet of Goering's vultures with orders to shoot down the British troops like cattle. Never! Never in all God's world as long as there was an R.A.F. plane left, and an R.A.F. pilot alive to fly it!

Suddenly Dave became conscious of a great pain in his right arm. He looked down to see Freddy gripping it tightly with one hand and pounding it with his other fist. The light of a mad man was in the English youth's eyes. When he had Dave's attention he stopped pounding and pointed to the left and beyond a short line of bomb blasted wharves.

"Look, look, Dave!" came his shrill scream faintly. "Look off that first wharf. There's a motor boat. It was trying to get in close, but a Messerschmitt came down and sprayed the chap at the wheel. See! He's trying to get up. And there's the Messerschmitt again. Dave! The tide will carry that boat up against those rocks, and smash in its bottom. Dave! Can you swim? We've got to reach that boat before it hits the rocks. Look! The Messerschmitt is shooting again. He's got the poor chap. He's got him this time!"

As Freddy screamed in his ear Dave looked out at the boat. It was a long slinky looking power boat, but it wasn't even slinking along, now. The lone figure had fallen across the engine hood, and a diving Messerschmitt was hammering more bullets into his body. And a running tide was carrying the craft broadside toward some jagged rocks that stuck up out of the water not two hundred yards away.

Dave was looking at it. And then suddenly he realized that his feet were pounding across the beach. That he was racing madly down the beach toward the water's edge. And that Freddy Farmer was close at his heels.

CHAPTER NINETEEN

The White Cliffs!

By the time they reached the water they had stripped off their hospital jackets, torn free their water canteens, and flung them away. Shoulder to shoulder they splashed out as far as they could, then dived in. They broke surface together and struck out for the helpless craft being carried toward its doom by the tide. Above them raged another mighty battle of the air. Bombs fell close and when one struck the water and went off, a thousand fists seemed to hammer against their chests. Behind them the flames of Dunkirk leaped high, and the glow turned the waters through which they swam to the color of blood. And there ahead of them was the sleek-looking motorboat, like a highly polished brown log drifting on the crest of a shimmering red sea.

A great fire burned in Dave's lungs, and his arms became like bars of lead that required every remaining ounce of his strength to lift up and cut down into the water again. But he fought back the aches, and the pains, and the gnawing fatigue. And so did Freddy Farmer there by his side. They kept their eyes fixed on that drifting motorboat and they didn't take them off it until after what seemed like years they were alongside it and hooking an arm over the gunwale. For a moment they just hung there panting and gulping for air. Then at an unspoken signal they each shifted their grip to the small brass rail that ran along each side from stem to stern, and hauled themselves into the boat.

Not even then did they speak a word, for words were unnecessary, now. There was a job to do, and a job to be done fast. The rocks weren't more than sixty yards away. Shaking water from his face, Dave leaped toward the engine hood, lifted up the motionless bullet riddled body and lowered it gently to the deck. At the same time Freddy caught up an oar and rushed toward the bow to fend off the craft should it reach the rocks.

Lifting the engine hood Dave took one look inside and gulped with relief. Messerschmitt bullets had not touched the American built engine. A quick glance down at the priming can in the dead man's stiff hand told Dave he had been trying to start the engine when the Messerschmitt first dived. Perhaps he had throttled too much, and stalled the engine. There was no way of knowing that, and no time to wonder about it. If there was something else wrong, and the priming can didn't do the trick, then he and Freddy could at least save the boat from being slammed up against the rocks.

It was time for Lady Luck to smile again, however. Dave primed the engine, and stepped on the starter pedal, and the engine roared up instantly in full throated song. He leaped for the wheel, yanked back the throttle, and then swung the wheel over hard. The rudder bit into the water, and the power boat slid by the jagged rocks with but a few feet to spare and glided out toward deep water.

"Made it!" Dave shouted wildly.

"Right-o!" Freddy yelled back from the bow. "This is one Herr Hitler doesn't get, by gosh. Not if *I* can help it! Oh, Dave, let's...."

"Me too!" Dave interrupted him. "I know what you're going to say. Let's go over and pick up as many of those fellows as we can! You're doggone right! Here we go!"

At that exact moment, however, the fates of war changed their plans. At that moment a steel fish made in Nazi land slid past the watchful eyes of a destroyer and let go a single torpedo straight into the maze of craft hovering off shore beneath the raging sky battle above. True, only one torpedo. And even as it streaked out from its tube the eyes aboard the destroyer saw it, and the destroyer's guns spoke ... and there was one U-boat less. However, one torpedo was on its way. And it slammed into the bow of a sturdy coastal vessel plodding out to the center of the Channel.

In the blaze of light that spewed up from the side of the vessel Dave saw the decks crowded with khaki clad soldiers. Then they were lost to view as the vessel heeled way over and was engulfed in a mighty cloud of smoke. No sooner had what his eyes seen registered oh his brain than he hauled down hard on the wheel and pulled the motor boat's bow away from the shore and out toward that floating cloud of smoke and dull red flame.

Other boats did the same thing, but Dave and Freddy were closer than any of the others, and they reached there first. Killing his speed as much as possible Dave worked the craft inch by inch toward the cluster of heads that were now bobbing out from under the edge of the cloud of smoke. Then when he was real close he throttled all the way back and let go of the wheel and raced with Freddy to the stern of the boat. They grabbed the first hand stretched up toward them and pulled the dripping figure into the boat. No sooner was he in than they let him shift for himself and grabbed for the next outstretched hand. Then another, and another, and another, until there were no more bobbing heads close to them.

By then other craft had arrived and were picking up survivors from that doomed vessel. As Dave straightened up he stared out across the water just in time to see the last bit of the vessel's bow slide down below the waves and disappear. One look and then he was pushing through the soldiers he and Freddy had rescued, to the wheel at the bow bulkhead. Cheers and praise filled his ears but he was too all in to even so much as grin. And, also, memory of that U-boat was still fresh in his mind. If one slipped past, why not two, or even three? Dunkirk was behind him, and a sky battle was raging high above him, but he did not know what might be lurking in the waters under him. The sooner he got the boat away, the better it would be for all concerned.

He reached the wheel at the same time Freddy did. And hardly realizing it, both grabbed hold. Dave shot out his other hand and opened up the throttle. Together, as one man, they guided the power boat in and around the other rescue craft until they were clear and heading straight out into the Channel. Once there was nothing but open water ahead of them they both relaxed, looked into each other's eyes and grinned.

"Well, that *must* be the last surprise, Freddy," Dave said. "There just isn't anything else that could happen that would startle me."

"Nor me, either!" Freddy breathed. "The excitement's all over for us, now. In another hour we'll be in England."

And then suddenly a hand was clapped down on each of them, and a hoarse voice boomed,

"Well, of all things! You two!"

They both spun around, then stopped dead and gasped in bewildered amazement. There standing in his water-soaked uniform was General Caldwell, Chief of British Staff. His piercing black eyes bored into theirs, and his teeth showed white in a broad smile.

"Good heavens, you, General!" Dave finally managed to gulp out. "Why, I didn't even know we'd hauled you aboard!"

"But you did, and thank God for that!" the General said fervently. "And do you know, it's the strangest thing ever! I was telling the captain of that boat about how you stole that plane, when the blasted torpedo struck. By gad, it's incredible. But how in the world did you get here? and in this boat, too!"

"Later, sir, if you don't mind," Freddy spoke up and put a hand on the General's sleeve. "Please tell us the truth. We've got to know. The information we gave you wasn't any help? You got it too late?"

General Caldwell stared at him hard, and then shook his head.

"You're dead wrong, Freddy, if you think that," he said in his oddly soft voice. "I spoke the truth to you in the Lille hospital. Look back there, both of you."

They turned and with their eyes followed the General's finger pointing at the beach at Dunkirk.

"That's the last of the British Army to leave France," he spoke again. "We've been getting them out for days, and against terrific odds. The only reason I was on that boat that was torpedoed, instead of being back there to be the last man to leave, was because I had my orders to return at once and start getting things reorganized. But they will all be in England before this fog gives the Stukas the chance they want. And praise to dear God for the fog and the rain he has sent us in these days of heroic effort. But, what I am trying to say to you, is this. Had I not received your information in time, thousands upon thousands of those brave chaps would never have been able to reach Dunkirk in time to be taken off. They would now be trapped in France and in Belgium. No, boys, it was not too late. And to you two England owes a debt she will never be able to repay."

"I'm glad," Freddy whispered softly. "I'm glad it was not too late."

"Gosh, me too," Dave mumbled, and tried to say more but the words wouldn't come.

And so the three of them: two boys and the General stood there with their faces turned toward England while the boat cut through the dawn-greyed swells and the light fog. And then after a long time the fog lifted and they saw it there ahead.

"Dover!" Freddy said in a choked voice, and tears trickled down his cheeks. "The chalk cliffs of Dover. England!"

"Yes, the chalk cliffs of Dover, and England," General Caldwell murmured huskily. "We've taken a pretty bad beating, but it's far from being all over. We may even take some more beatings. Perhaps several of them. But in the end we will win. We must win, for there will always be an England. Always!"

Three days after the world-thrilling evacuation of Dunkirk, Dave Dawson sat in the living-room of Freddy Farmer's house in Baker Street in London. Freddy was there, of course, and so was his dad. And so was Dave's father. Within an hour after touching English soil the British War Office had contacted Dave's dad in Paris where he had gone hoping to pick up the trail of his missing son. And, now, the four of them were waiting because of a phone call from General Caldwell. A phone call stating that the Chief of Staff was on his way there, and for them all please to wait.

"Boy, I wish he'd get here!" Dave exclaimed for the umpteenth time.

"He didn't say why he wanted to see us?" Freddy asked his father for the umpteenth time, too.

"No, Freddy," the senior Farmer replied patiently. "He didn't say a word about it."

"Gee, do I hope, do I hope, *do I hope!*" Dave breathed and pressed his two clenched fists together. "Do I hope he has fixed it for us to get into the R.A.F., even though we are a bit under age. He said he'd do everything he could. And, Dad?"

Dave turned and looked into his father's face.

"Yes, Dave?"

"I sure hope it really *is* okay with you," Dave said. "I mean getting into the R.A.F., if I possibly can. It's.... Well, it's just that nothing else seems important now, except trimming the pants off the Nazis. And I want to help, no matter *what*kind of help it is."

"I understand, perfectly, Dave," his father said with a smile. "I know exactly how you feel, because I feel the same way. I'm staying over here to help, too. In the government end of things."

Dave's exclamation of surprise was cut short by the ringing of the door bell. Freddy's father answered it and came back into the room with General Caldwell. The Chief of Staff greeted them all and then handed Dave and Freddy each a small package.

"And with life-long gratitude from the bottom of my heart," he said gravely.

They opened the packages to find an expensive wrist watch in each. And on the back of each watch was the inscription:

To One Of The Two Finest And Bravest
Boys I Ever Met
General H. V. K. Caldwell

"And, now, the real reason I came here," the General said before they could even begin to blurt out their thanks and appreciation. "Their Majesties, King George and Queen Elizabeth, are waiting to receive you at Buckingham Palace. And your fathers, of course."

"The King ... and the Queen?" Freddy said in a hushed voice.

"Oh boy, meeting the King and Queen in Buckingham Palace!" Dave breathed. And then he couldn't hold it any longer. "General Caldwell!" the words rushed off his lips. "What Freddy and I asked you about? I mean ... the R.A.F. Is there any chance?"

The General tried to look stern, but he just couldn't keep the grin from breaking through.

"Among other things," he said in his soft voice, "Their Majesties wish to be the first to congratulate their two new members of the Royal Air Force. So, I suggest we do not keep them waiting, eh?"

Dave and Freddy looked at each other without speaking, but their eyes spoke volumes. The dream had come true. Or perhaps it was only beginning. Either way, though, one thing was certain. Beginning with this moment they would have the chance to do their share as pilots of the Royal Air Force in the battle for Britain. And that chance was all they asked. Nothing more.

——THE END——

See next page.

A Page from

DAVE DAWSON WITH THE R.A.F.

At that moment a short, savage burst from Flight Lieutenant Barton-Woods' guns snapped Dave's eyes back to the Junkers. They were still quite a ways off but the Green Flight leader had let go with a challenging burst hoping that the Germans would give up thoughts of escape and turn back to give battle. However, it was instantly obvious that the Junkers pilots and their crews didn't want any truck with three Spitfire pilots. The nose of each ship was pushed down a bit to add speed to the get away attempt. And a moment later Dave saw the flash of sunlight on bombs dropping harmlessly down into the rolling grey-green swells where the Channel blends in with the North Sea.

"Not this day, my little Jerries!" Flight Lieutenant Barton-Woods' voice boomed over the radio. "Let's make the beggars pay for dropping bombs in our Channel, Green Flight! Give it to them!"

The last was more or less the signal that each pilot was on his own. Dave waited until he saw his flight leader swerve off to slam in at the Junkers to the right. Then he touched rudder, and with Freddy sticking right with him, swerved off after the other German raider.

61171422R00089

Made in the USA
Middletown, DE
17 August 2019